SECRETS AT CITY HOSPITAL

Spilt coffee, broken-down car, laddered tights — Rachel's first day on duty as Registrar in the busy maternity department at City Hospital could hardly have started worse! Thrown in at the deep end with an emergency to deal with, the last thing she needs is the spark of attraction she feels for capable male midwife Grant. She's given up on relationships, but she can't help falling for Grant, even though it becomes clear he's hiding something . . .

Books by Kate Allan
in the Linford Romance Library:

FATEFUL DECEPTION
THE RESTLESS HEART
THE SMUGGLER RETURNS

KATE ALLAN

SECRETS AT CITY HOSPITAL

Complete and Unabridged

LINFORD
Leicester

First published in Great Britain in 2011

First Linford Edition
published 2012

British Library CIP Data

Allan, Kate.
   Secrets at City Hospital. - -
(Linford romance library)
   1. Love stories.
   2. Large type books.
   I. Title II. Series
   823.9'2–dc23

   ISBN 978–1–4448–1214–5

Published by
F. A. Thorpe (Publishing)
Anstey, Leicestershire

Set by Words & Graphics Ltd.
Anstey, Leicestershire
Printed and bound in Great Britain by
T. J. International Ltd., Padstow, Cornwall

This book is printed on acid-free paper

1

Dr Rachel Booth, Registrar. She touched the batch of small barcoded stickers someone had placed on her desk. She'd finally made it — she'd got the coveted Registrar post in busy City Hospital's maternity department. Perhaps the day would get better from here on? It certainly couldn't get much worse . . . She picked up the telephone.

'Hello? Is that City Garage?' she said into the receiver. 'You picked up my car this morning; it wouldn't start. The guy couldn't fix it so you towed it away.' She picked up a pen and started fiddling with it while she waited for the reception-ist to come back with an answer. 'Oh — okay. I'll ring back later this after-noon, then.'

She put the phone down. They didn't know what was wrong. Great! Now it looked as if she'd be getting an expensive cab home tonight after all.

Not only had the car refused to start but she'd managed to knock her coffee off the breakfast table, and then laddered her tights as she scrambled around with the dustpan and brush. There was nothing like looking smart on your first day in a new job, but she had given up on the whole idea of a skirt and heels and had hastily pulled on a very plain pair of black trousers and flats. Perhaps someone was trying to tell her something?

'Mmm, real coffee,' Rachel murmured to herself, sipping from the plastic take-away cup. She'd had time to go to Cafe Alberto, the coffee shop on the ground floor and her clinic didn't start for half an hour, so she was just about to enjoy her coffee when her pager beeped.

'What? How can anyone possibly know I'm here? I've only been in the job a few hours!' She pulled the pager out of her bag to turn it off.

Bettina Holland, one of the F2s

— second year medical students — who shared the second desk in the office Rachel was in, looked up from her paperwork. 'Shall I go?'

'Thanks, but I'd better assume they actually do want a Registrar.' Rachel had known Bettina for less than twenty minutes, but clearly she was one of the keen ones. Rachel gathered herself together quickly. *And I really must stop talking to myself!* she thought as she closed the door behind her.

She only needed to go up one flight of stairs and through two sets of double-doors to be in the labour ward, if she remember correctly. She walked to the end of the corridor, through the doors — and ended up in the hospital's central atrium. Wrong! She retraced her steps, found the stairs then the second set of double-doors and bingo! The sign on the doors said, LABOUR WARD.

She waved her keycard at the scanner and walked into a sea of familiar chaos. Midwives rushed past, coming in and out of doors. A porter was calling for help as he wheeled a woman in an advanced stage of labour into a side room. Another midwife was trying to move a woman down the corridor who was walking very slowly and moaning. The only midwife left on the station was deep in conversation on the telephone.

A very petite Chinese midwife grabbed her arm. 'Are you Registrar?' she said in broken English.

'Yes. Dr Rachel Booth. Did you beep me?'

'Come quick, doctor. We need you see lady.'

Rachel was relieved to see a senior midwife in the side room looking at the tracing that was being taken before she tore the sheet off and handed it to Rachel. 'This is Laura. She's been on the drip now for eight hours but there's been no progress in the last four. I did an examination about half an hour ago and she was still at four centimetres.'

'Thank you,' Rachel said and looked at the tracing. The baby's heartbeat was decelerating at regular intervals; not a good sign. He could be reacting to the drip, or there could be any number of other reasons for his distress.

She looked at the patient. She was young, certainly no more than twenty, and there was no partner in the room.

'First baby?' Rachel asked. The girl nodded, looking decidedly uncomfortable and hot. There was a rap at the door, someone saying the senior midwife was needed elsewhere, and when Rachel looked around to see if the Chinese midwife would take the patient's temperature, she had also disappeared. *So, I'll do it myself then*, she thought.

Rachel smiled at the patient. 'I'm just going to take your temperature.' Not that there were any thermometers on the trolley . . . or in any of the cupboards . . . 'Sorry, I'll be back in less than a minute.'

The patient looked alarmed and let out a cry. Rachel glanced at the tracing coming out of the machine. Another contraction.

'Are you here by yourself?' Rachel asked and wondered why the girl hadn't been given an epidural for the pain. It was usually a good idea to get the epidural in before starting an induction drip, because the drip could result in extremely painful contractions.

'My Mum is here but she went for something to eat,' the girl said, breathing deeply. She seemed to be coping well enough, but Rachel looked around for the patient's notes, a little concerned.

She touched the girl's hand and smiled. 'I really will be back in a minute. I need a thermometer and can't seem to find one here.' *And your notes*, she thought to herself. A midwife had probably taken them away and then left them at the station.

The corridor was surprisingly quiet, although Rachel could hear plenty of bustle coming from the side rooms. The midwifes' station was empty so she started looking through the trays.

'Excuse me?' A deep, male voice

came from behind her. She turned and looked up to see a very handsome nose, a chiselled chin and two dark brown eyes.

'Can I help you?' he said. 'Or should I just leave you rifling through hospital property?'

'I work here.' She stood up, not caring if he was a doctor, a hospital manager or the post boy. She needed some help.

'Ah . . . I didn't see your card, sorry.'

'That's okay. I'm the new Registrar. Listen, I have a patient in labour — '

'Well, this is the Labour Ward . . . '

'Yes, I scc, vcry funny. But right now I need a thermometer and her notes. They're not with her.'

He pulled a disposable thermometer from the top pocket of his overalls. 'First of your problems solved.'

Rachel blinked, putting two and two together: the blue overalls with white piping; his manner. 'Wait a minute, you're a midwife?'

'Men can be midwives, just as they've

allowed women to be doctors.' There was a touch of ice in his voice. She'd probably touched a sore spot.

Today just kept getting better . . . 'I'm sorry,' she said. 'It's my first day, new hospital, I'm in at the deep end somewhat.' Rachel took a deep breath.

'Who's the patient?' He had a slight accent she couldn't place.

'The girl in Room Eight. Laura . . . er . . . '

'Williams.'

'Laura Williams. Right.' She ventured a small smile.

'I'm on it,' he told her, all efficiency. 'I'll bring the notes through as soon as I've found them.'

'Oh. Thank you.'

'You go back to her, then, and I'll stay here and find her notes.' He was speaking to her as if she was a child, but strangely she found it almost reassuring. Perhaps he was one of those port-in-a-storm types. Not a bad quality to have if you were a midwife.

Rachel hurried back to her patient.

The mother hadn't returned yet and, as she suspected, Laura's temperature was raised. 'You may have an infection,' she said.

Laura looked wild-eyed. Rachel sat down beside her and explained, 'There's no need to be worried. There's no immediate emergency but I do think we should talk about having the baby delivered.'

'You mean by C-section?'

'Yes.'

'But I don't want to have an operation,' Laura wailed. 'I want to have my baby naturally.'

'We have to think about the safety of you and your baby, Laura. If your labour isn't progressing I would strongly recommend we go for a section.'

'No!' Laura cried out. 'Where's my Mum? I want my Mum!' She started sobbing gently.

Where was her mother, indeed? Rachel wondered what to do. Neither of the midwives had returned and this girl really needed someone in here all the time to keep an eye on the baby's heartbeat. The patient also needed to be talked into having a C-section. Rachel took Laura's hand. 'Really, I do feel it is the best thing to do.'

'Go away!' Laura jerked her hand away.

Labour was an emotionally difficult time as well as being physically challenging. Poor girl. But Rachel knew that the good thing was that as soon as baby arrived, the new mother would be smiling and starting to forget the ordeal she'd just been through.

She busied herself looking at the tracing and remained at a loss what to do. Thankfully, within a couple of minutes there was a knock on the door. The mother, hopefully, or senior midwife. It was Mr Male Midwife himself — and he was empty-handed. Rachel frowned.

'I've looked high and low.' He grimaced and she couldn't help thinking how attractive he looked even wearing such an expression. 'They're not at the station. Shall I have a look in here?'

'Please do,' Rachel replied distract-edly, not making any move from studying the tracing from the baby monitor.

'And thank you too, Dr . . . ?'

'Booth,' she snapped. He might look like Patrick Dempsey but he could get off his high horse.

'Grant Mackenzie, midwife.'

'Sorry,' she said, feeling a little bad now as she realised she had been a little offhand. 'Thank you for looking for the notes.' Now where was the senior midwife? She wasn't even aware yet of the protocols here regarding transfer-ring a patient to theatre.

Laura cried out and immediately Grant Mackenzie was at her side and asking, 'On a scale of one to five, where five's being run over by a bus, how painful was that one?'

'Four . . . Three . . . Four . . . I dunno.'

'Has someone explained about gas and air to help with the pain?' His voice was so gentle, Rachel found herself feeling more relaxed too.

'Tried that, made me sick,' Laura gasped.

The door opened — at last, the girl's mother! A short woman with dark hair and carrying a knitting bag full of women's magazines came bustling over to the bed. 'Laura, Laura,' she cooed as she sat in the chair at the side.

Grant Mackenzie withdrew to consult the trace and Rachel joined him.

'I've been qualified for three months and I know what I'm doing.' He raised an eyebrow. 'In case you're wondering.'

'Might I have a word?' Rachel gritted her teeth, leaned over his broad shoulders and spoke in a low voice. 'I think she needs to go into theatre — '

'Well, if you think she needs to go to theatre, you're the registrar.'

Rachel caught a faint whiff of his cologne. It was a strangely old-fashioned spicy scent, not sexy . . . well, maybe. She looked at the span of his shoulders. Definitely maybe. Ah, who was she kidding.

'So?' he said, snapping her out of her reverie.

Sometimes she wished she worked in a nice, simple job in an office where people's lives weren't at risk and where she could cultivate her repartee and give as good as she got. But here it just wasn't her style.

'I'm so new here I don't how to get a patient into theatre,' she said.

'We have a system here — it's brilliantly simple.' He smiled.

'What's that?'

'If the doctor says yes then it's go, go go. You're a doctor. Say yes and I'll go and make that call.' He gestured towards the door.

'Except that the patient doesn't want to go into theatre.' Rachel sighed. 'I'd better do an exam first.'

'If you like, but I wouldn't bother,' he said, adding, 'Look at this.' He pointed out two occasions on the tracing where the baby's heartbeat had slowed significantly.

Rachel knew she had to act quickly. 'Okay. Please turn the drip off.'

'Sure thing.' Grant turned around

13

and got to work.

'Laura?' Rachel prised the girl's attention away from her mother. 'I'm afraid that your baby is showing signs of distress and we can no longer continue your drip. Our only real alternative at this stage is to deliver by section.' Laura gave a wail. 'Do you understand me?'

'Nooooo,' Laura cried out.

'There, there, love, it's for the best,' her mother soothed.

Rachel really wished she had the patient's notes. It was difficult to know whether she was really making the right decision. 'If in doubt, safety first' had been the motto of her consultant in her first student rotation in obstetrics. Always better to be safe than sorry.

'Mum, have you got my lip balm?'

Rachel bit back a smile. Within half an hour this girl would have the ultimate joy of becoming a mother and top of her mind right now was lip balm. Having said that, it was very dry in the room.

Laura's mum rummaged in her bag.

'Oh, what's this?' She pulled out a sheaf of maternity notes. 'I must have picked up your notes with my magazines,' she said sheepishly.

'Thank you.' Rachel took them and read quickly . . . normal pregnancy, normal niggles, nothing unusual . . . blood pressure fine . . . labour had been induced because the baby was now seventeen days late. But Rachel knew that these indications were unpredictable and often didn't work and some babies just reacted badly to the induction drip.

It seemed quite a straightforward case. First day on the job, first baby.

'I'm not having my baby cut out,' Laura said between contractions.

'You don't have to go to theatre,' Grant said and Rachel realised his slight accent was Scottish. She still felt like hitting him, though. 'But then you might end up staying here for days . . . a week . . . no food, no baby.'

Seemed she'd pre-judged him too soon.

'He's right, love,' the girl's mother

said. 'Your little one's just too comfort-able in there.'

* * *

Half an hour later Rachel came out of theatre where she'd stayed to watch the healthy eight-pound baby being deliv-ered by her new colleagues. Buoyed up by the sheer joy of it, she'd completely forgotten she had an afternoon clinic. Luckily it was consultant-led as it was for high-risk mothers so she would only be stepping in to lead if the consultant was away — which Professor Gatiss wasn't, thankfully.

It was nearly five o'clock by the time they'd seen the last clinic patient and she made it to Cafe Alberto. She could really have done with the caffeine hours ago; it had been a long day, but still, better late than never.

'A tall Americano, please,' she told the barista and the coffee machine snorted and hissed.

'How about a tall Scotsman?' Grant

Mackenzie had somehow appeared in the queue directly behind her. And he *was* tall; at least six foot.

Suddenly conscious that she must look a mess, she pushed her various strands of stray hair behind her ears. Was he flirting with her? She wasn't sure how she felt about that.

'So how was your first day?'

'It started badly but then got better,' she replied.

'That must have been because of meeting mc, then.' He beamed at her.

He was flirting! Rachel felt suddenly awkward. 'Excuse me. I have to go,' she said, starting to walk away. She couldn't deal with this now, not Mr Patrick Dempsey-lookalike, the comedy male midwife.

'Catch you later.' He raised his hand to call her back. 'You'll not be wanting that Americano, then?'

Gosh, she was such an idiot! The barista had just placed the take-away coffee she'd ordered and paid for down on the counter. She turned on her heels and collected it, then hurried out of the shop.

2

Rachel handed over a ten-pound note to the taxi driver and told him to keep the change. Just as well she'd got a pay rise with the new post. Her mobile beeped with a text message from her sister, Becky: *Call me when you have a minute*. She let herself in the communal door and climbed the three flights of stairs to her top floor flat.

Her flat was in a rather attractive low-rise development that overlooked a canal wharf, and she'd agreed to rent it at first sight. Not that her flat overlooked the water — unless you endangered yourself by leaning over the balcony — but still, this was home for the past three weeks and the foreseeable future. She'd had enough of suburbia. There was a single bar and restaurant at the wharf and it only got busy on Friday and Saturday nights, but she rather liked the noise, the sounds of people enjoying themselves. Somehow their shrieks and laughter late at night made her feel a little less lonely.

Rachel kicked off her shoes, poured herself a glass of red wine and slumped down on the sofa. Now all she needed was a hairy hound to fetch her slippers . . . or a man.

She yawned. She'd better ring her sister before it got too late and she forgot. It was thoughtful of her to enquire how her first day went. Uncharacteristically thoughtful, in fact.

'Hello!' Becky squealed. 'You're free to talk, are you? You're not in theatre or something?'

'No, I'm at home,' Rachel said wearily. 'Since when have I ever called you from theatre?'

'They do it all the time in Holby City. Someone else holds the phone to the consultant's ear when they're right in the middle of the critical part of a heart operation.'

'Not in real life.' Rachel smiled. What

did her sister, in her easy office job, know about the sharp end of medicine, apart from what she watched on the television? 'Anyway my first day went okay, thanks for asking.'

'Was it your first day today? Oh, Sis, I forgot — sorry.' Some things never changed, Rachel thought. 'Anyway,' Becky continued. 'Are you free this evening? Can I pop over in a little while?'

'Sure.' Rachel was a little taken aback. Although they now lived in the same city, she'd not seen her sister since first moving back here. Her sister's boyfriend Jamie had shown up to help her move some boxes. Not that he'd really been needed, as the removal men had done an excellent job, but still, the thought was nice.

As for Becky herself, she'd not actually seen her for a couple of months. 'Yes, that would great,' she replied, in spite of her tiredness. 'I think I have a bottle of wine in the fridge. Are you coming alone?'

'Jamie's working late actually, so yes. Good, I'm so glad I can come over. I'll be with you in about half an hour, okay?'

'You have my address?'

'Yes, yes.'

The line went dead and Rachel peered at the phone for a moment before pushing the button to end the call, wondering what her sister could possibly be so excited about.

★ ★ ★

Three-quarters of an hour later, the door buzzer went. Rachel opened the door to let her sister in . . . and stopped . . . and stared. There could be no doubt. No! She couldn't be . . .

'Surprise!' Becky beamed and threw her arms around her sister. 'You're going to be an auntie!'

'I . . . I can't believe you didn't tell me.' Rachel grappled for something to say. She couldn't believe it. Becky was four years younger than her and she wasn't even married. Jamie was nice, but . . .

'Why are you frowning?' Becky drew away.

'It's Jamie's?'

'Of course it's Jamie's, you daft cushion! And before you ask, Ms Prim-and-Proper, no we're not getting married, at least, not yet. We have enough on our plate with the baby and everything. Look . . . ' Becky fished around in her handbag. 'I had the scan today. Oh, where's the photo gone . . . ?'

'At City Hospital?'

'No, we're not in City's catchment area, so I went to Granby General.'

'You have a choice, you know. You can request City. Just tell your GP.'

'Do you want to see a picture of your niece or nephew, or what?' Becky held the envelope close to her chest.

'Yes, of course I do.' Rachel took a deep breath. She needed to hold herself together and not be a dampener on Becky's excitement. She took the black and white blurry scan photo, which looked exactly like a thousand scan photos she'd seen before. 'How wonderful. Wait until the twenty-week scan and you'll be able to see so much more.'

'I know that.' Becky's forehead puckered into a frown. 'Just because I'm not a doctor doesn't mean I don't know anything about pregnancy.'

'Would you like something to drink?' Rachel said evasively.

'Don't change the subject.' Becky took the photo back, sat down and folded her arms in front of her. 'You just don't like it, because you wish you were the one having a baby. Go on, admit it. The sooner we clear the air, the better. Look, Sis, I need you to be happy for me. Really.'

The look in Becky's eyes was like a sorrowful puppy. Rachel wiped away a tear with the back of her sleeve.

'I am happy for you, Becks, but, you know, it's . . . hard.'

Becky sprang up and hugged her. Boy, she needed that hug. 'Don't leave it so long again, Becks,' she muttered.

If her first day had dragged, her first week simply flew by.

This morning had started quietly and Bettina had fetched them coffees. Rachel had marked her down as rather quiet and unassuming, but now she stood in front of Rachel's desk with a coffee cup in each hand and a determined look on her face. 'Dr Booth?'

'Yes? And do call me Rachel.'

'Rachel, then . . . because we've been short of a Registrar, I've not seen as much as I would have liked on this rotation.' Bettina bit her lip.

'Have you ever sat in on the diabetic mothers clinic?' Rachel took a long gulp of her Americano as Bettina shook her head. 'No? Well, I'm taking it this morning in Mr Larsson's absence.'

Indeed she'd been doing the clinics every day for the last three days while Professor Larsson attended a conference in South Africa. In some ways, a baptism of fire; in others, so much was

24

routine that she'd welcome an F2, and a keen one at that, in with her.

They'd already seen four diabetic mothers at various stages of their pregnancies before a tall, slim, dark-haired woman came into the room.

'Amie LeFevre?' Rachel opened up the notes and the woman nodded. 'Please take a seat. I'm Rachel Booth, Registrar, taking the clinic today for Mr Larsson. This is Bettina Holland, student doctor, is that all right?' The woman nodded again then Rachel went on, 'How far are you now . . . ?'

'Thirty-five weeks.' Amie had a heavy French accent.

'And how have you been feeling?'

'A little tired.' Amie shrugged. 'But that is normal, is it not?'

'Yes, it is. Have you brought your sample?'

Amie produced a small pot from her handbag.

'Bettina, would you take Amie's blood pressure while I check her sample?' Rachel pulled a fresh pair of gloves on and began to test the urine. 'I'm just checking for proteins,' she explained to the patient. 'I'm sure you've had this done at every check-up.'

It was marginal, but there appeared to be a trace of protein, which could be caused by the diabetes, or it might be an infection, or . . . ? Rachel checked through the patient's notes. Previous samples in the patient's pregnancy had all been clear.

Bettina was using the electronic blood pressure monitor and frowning.

'Best to do it manually,' Rachel suggested kindly. The electronic machines could be unreliable.

Bettina got the manual blood pressure unit down from the shelf, wound the cuff around Amie's upper arm and put her stethoscope into her ears to listen. Again a crease appeared on her brow.

'Better try again,' Rachel advised.

Bettina smiled thinly. 'I'm probably not doing it right. Sorry.'

'Medical school these days, I don't

know . . . shall I do it?' Rachel kept her tone very light as she noticed the patient beginning to look concerned. Bettina nodded gratefully.

Rachel got 160 over 105 — sky high. No wonder Bettina had thought she was doing something wrong. Rachel jotted the measurement down in the notes and looked back over the patient's history . . . 120 over 90 or thereabouts every time, so 160 over 105 was way out of line.

'Have you had any headaches recently, or blurred vision?'

'No.' Amie shook her head.

'Any shortness of breath?' Rachel persisted.

'No, nothing unusual,' Amie answered.

'Would you like to hop up onto the bed and we'll have a listen to baby?' Rachel smiled, but she was likely to have to admit Amie to the Day Assessment Unit. If her blood pressure came down again today, then great, but if it was a permanent fixture it could be an indicator of trouble, especially if there were

27

any signs of swelling.

The baby seemed fine and Rachel was pleased not to discover any noticeable swelling. She broke the news to Amie that she should stay in for a few hours and explained that her high blood pressure and trace of protein in her urine could be indicators of a dangerous condition called pre-eclampsia. They needed to be on the safe side.

Alarm crossed Amie's face as she spoke.

'Really, we are just being cautious,' Rachel assured her. 'Is there anyone you'd like to call? You can use the phone here if you like.' She turned to Bettina and asked, 'Could you go and organise a bed?'

Amie made the call to her husband while Rachel filled in her paperwork. They had both finished just as Bettina returned, looking a little flustered.

'Dr Booth . . . Rachel, could I have a word?' Rachel followed her back out into the corridor. 'Day Assessment say they have no beds.'

'What?'

'They've had referrals this morning straight from Casualty.'

'Great.' Rachel clicked her pen shut and placed it in her pocket. 'Well, I'm not sending Amie home. We'll have to admit her to antenatal.'

Bettina raised an eyebrow. It wasn't an ideal situation as the whole purpose of the Day Assessment Unit was to save the antenatal ward from having to deal with cases like these.

Rachel had to make a decision. 'Hang on, let me speak to them and see what's going on up there. If there's a bed coming up soon, perhaps I can put my name on it and in the meantime we'll send Amie to Outpatients for a blood test so that'll already be done.'

Feeling in control again, she smiled at Bettina and added, 'Give me five minutes to make the call while you stay here with the patient and practise your bedside manner.'

Rachel popped into an empty con-sulting room across the corridor and picked up the phone.

'Day Assessment Unit.' It was a man's voice and strangely familiar. Could it be Grant Mackenzie? Rachel frowned.

'Hello? Day Assessment Unit?' he repeated with his light Scottish burr.

'This is Dr Rachel Booth,' she said briskly. There was silence. 'I have a patient who needs careful monitoring.' Rachel bit her lip. 'But I understand you're full?' Silence. Rachel felt the hairs on the back of her neck prickle. She tried to sound as casual as she could. 'And I wondered if you might have a bed becoming available any time soon?'

'Hmmm, a bed you say?'

Yes, a bed! Rachel wanted to shout. Really, this wasn't the time for humour. She had Amie and a whole waiting room of outpatients to deal with.

'Okay, that I can do,' he said eventually.

She felt suddenly nervous having this conversation, which she couldn't understand at all. 'Are you sure? Dr Holland called a couple of minutes ago and was told you were full.'

'Well, she didn't speak to me. I've got a lady who's just come in for an hour's monitoring. In fact she might even have gone home already.'

'Great, brilliant. My patient is diabetic, thirty-five weeks and has come in presenting abnormally high blood pressure with traces of protein in her urine.' Rachel passed on Amie's details.

'I'd admit her to antenatal if I were you,' he said. 'You know we'll just end up referring her to antenatal if her BP doesn't come down in a couple of hours, and the chance of her BP just being an erratic measurement sounds slim, given the history.'

'Thank you for your informed opinion,' Rachel snapped, ignoring the fact that what he said was true and that Amie was destined most likely at least for an overnight stay.

'Okay, okay.' Mr Male Midwife sounded contrite. 'Send her right up, then. Catch you later.' The receiver clicked down.

What did he mean, *Catch you later?*

Rachel shook her head as she walked back to her consulting room but there remained the tiniest niggle that Mr Male Midwife had been flirting with her — and that thought made her feel shivery all over.

Pull yourself together, she told herself. The last thing she wanted or needed right now was a romance of any description. She fiddled with her watch strap. She had this new job to get to grips with — and, besides, she'd had it with men for a long, long time.

⋆ ⋆ ⋆

It was three in the afternoon by the time Rachel was able to take a break. She was half-way to Cafe Alberto when she had the sudden urge to make up an excuse to go upstairs to the Day Assessment Unit.

She turned around; she didn't need an excuse — she'd not really had a chance to take a look around there beyond the brief tour another doctor had given her. She reminded herself that she was a registrar here, she could go where she liked.

She could hear her heart beating as she swiped her card to open the double doors to the unit. It didn't calm down as she walked in. It was a small unit, just two bays with three beds in each, but it was unusual that it was full.

The only midwife in sight was dark-haired but certainly not Grant Mackenzie. She didn't look up from where she was sitting at the midwife's station doing paperwork. Rachel figured she could hardly go up to the midwife and ask for Grant Mackenzie without a proper excuse. Then again, loitering in the corridor might be problematic. She opened the door to the pantry and went inside.

And there Grant Mackenzie stood, leaning against the fridge with a mug of tea or coffee in his hand.

'Hello.' He looked surprised to see her.

'Hello.' There was an awkward silence. 'How's my patient?' Rachel asked. 'The diabetic mother.'

'Her BP's not come down so she'll certainly be in overnight.'

'Perhaps pre-eclampsia after all then,' Rachel muttered, and stared at the white boringness of the pantry fridge while she fought a sudden attack of shyness. For goodness' sake, he was just a midwife and work colleague!

'Considering the patient's a diabetic, I'd say it's a dead cert and put money on you delivering the baby within the week.'

It was true that a good proportion of diabetic mothers did develop pre-eclampsia. It was one of the main things to look out for. Rachel swept her gaze across him, from his very unsexy rubber work shoes to the top of his head. He was lean, but looked as if he worked out. 'You're well informed.'

'My brother was a doctor.' He shrugged and put his mug down on the worktop. She liked the way a half-smile played on his lips as he spoke.

So why aren't you a doctor? Rachel wanted to ask. But perhaps he'd tried and hadn't got the grades needed for medical school. It could be a touchy subject.

'About that drink, then?' He rubbed his hands together.

'What drink?' Rachel's mind raced but she was certain he'd not mentioned a drink before. Was he asking her out?

'You know, go for a drink after work perhaps?' He stuffed his hands in his pockets and sounded very casual.

'Oh, yes, well . . . ' Rachel stared at the floor. Was there a good reason not to get to know a colleague better over a drink after work? This wasn't a date, after all — or was it?

'What time do you finish?'

'You mean today?' Rachel looked up in surprise. He smiled broadly and she felt her legs go quivery.

'Why not? It's what colleagues do, isn't it?'

So it wasn't a date, then. Disappointment washed over her and she wanted to kick herself. 'Yes, that would be great.'

Date or not, of course she wasn't going to turn him down. Just being on the telephone to him made her senses sing, let alone being in the same room. But what was such a good-looking man doing working as a midwife? He should be in *Grey's Anatomy* on the television, not in City Hospital.

Actually, what she really wanted was at least two hours of prepping herself up, time for a long shower, time to put her make-up on properly, and time to dither about deciding what to wear . . . even if it wasn't a date.

3

Grant rested his forehead on the cold locker door. He clenched and unclenched his fists. Deep breaths. The image he'd just seen was stuck in his mind. The twenty-five-weeks pregnant mum being told that her baby would be stillborn, and no one could tell her why. The absolute pits. It didn't matter how many times he'd seen it, it never got any easier.

He wanted to go home, have a shower, switch the telly on, crack open a beer. Anything to try to numb his mind. Instead he was supposed to be taking the intriguing Dr Booth out for an after-work drink.

She was a strange one; haughty one minute, a near shambles the next, but he liked her. Oh, yes, he liked her and he'd like to get very close to her indeed. He couldn't remember the last time he'd had such an attraction to any woman at all, let alone one at work.

You'd have thought otherwise, being surrounded by so many women in midwifery, but he'd been so focussed on gaining the qualification he hadn't noticed. Perhaps he'd relaxed a bit now he was no longer a student. Actually he decided he was glad he was taking her out.

He pulled off his uniform and changed into jeans and a rugby shirt; not as smart as he'd be had it been planned, but at least he'd given his shoes a proper old-fashioned polish yesterday. He pulled a comb through his hair, splashed water on his face and finished with a dab of cologne to take away that peculiar smell of hospital.

'Hey, you smell nice.' Maria, a midwife who'd qualified at the same time as him, was hastening down the corridor holding an empty cardboard bed pan. 'Off on a hot date, then?'

'Perhaps,' Grant said.

'Then you are, then. Hope it goes badly — you know you and I were made for each other.' She blew him a kiss. She was an outrageous flirt but harmless, Grant considered. She was Spanish, dark and quite pretty, but he wasn't attracted to her; she was too flighty for him.

Quite unlike Dr Rachel Booth. There was a serious woman with many layers to her personality . . . layers that he longed to peel away so that he could reach the real woman, deep inside.

Rachel was waiting for him by the main hospital reception desk, wearing slacks and a blouse, her jacket hung over one arm. Frosty is how he'd describe her on the surface, but there was something about her, a fragility that drew him to her.

Bar Nova was only a block from the hospital, but not one of the places popular for hospital staff to go for drinks. It was stylish; all cream and chrome and wooden floors, with prices to match, and at this early time it was full of upscale office workers in suits. But not too full. He guided her to an empty table for two by the window. 'What would you like?'

'A dry white wine, please.'

'Pinot Grigio?'

'Yes, if they have it, or whatever you think would be good.'

At the bar he decided he might as well get a bottle and selected a promising looking Trebbiano. After all, he had all of tomorrow to sleep and lie-in before he started on a stretch of nights.

'You've been at City a week or so now?' he said, returning to their table.

A barman delivered a tiny bowl of olives and one of pretzels. Grant helped himself to a pretzel.

'Yes.' She seemed to be watching him closely.

He had another pretzel. 'Been out with a midwife before?'

'Funnily enough, no. Have you been out with a doctor?'

The barman returned with glasses and an ice bucket.

'I have, actually.' Grant grinned,

watching for her reaction. 'They all find me completely irresistible.' Her expression remained impassive. She blinked but she gave nothing away; she was wearing a mask. Well, he liked a challenge. The wine arrived and the waiter poured them both a glass.

'Very nice,' Rachel said, taking a sip. 'Although just one glass for me. My car's at the hospital. Where in Scotland are you from?'

Grant leaned back in his chair, relaxed. 'My, you're a serious lass. Do you ever let your hair down?' He took a mouthful of wine. 'Near Aberdeen.'

'How old are you?' Rachel fished around for topics of conversation.

'Thirty-two.' At least she was engaging with him, he supposed. Even if it did feel more like a job interview.

'Oh.' She raised her eyebrows. 'Then you're older than me. How come you've only just qualified in midwifery? What were you doing before?'

'I just lazed around.' He shifted in his seat. 'Learned a thing or two but mostly

I just wasted my time, although I'm a reformed character now.'

Actually he was glad they were talking like this. It made a welcome change from the usual flirtatious small talk. He took another gulp of wine. He was going to have to warm the situation up at some point, though.

'Tell me about you,' he said.

'There's nothing to tell. I went straight to medical school and now here I am. I grew up here, so I was excited when I saw the post advertised, and luckily Mr Larsson seemed to think I was the right candidate. So there we are.' She gave an attempt at a smile but folded her arms.

'You don't own ten stray cats or anything kooky like that?'

'They wouldn't be strays if I owned them.'

'Nothing passes you by, does it?' He suddenly saw in his head an imagined and an unbidden picture of her naked; not hard to imagine with her slim figure which the cut of her clothes showed off well. 'What am I thinking about now, then?' he challenged.

'Probably something . . . inappropriate.' She bit her lip. 'I can see the glint in your eye from here.'

'Ah, that's just a bit of dust. Let me whisper.' He pulled his chair around so he was beside her and leaned in to her ear and breathed so she'd feel it like the lightest of touches on her neck. His jaw clenched. How he wanted to take her and kiss her.

'I was just thinking about you . . . '

He heard her inhale. He shut his eyes momentarily, imagining her touch and it was an incredible effort not to kiss her here and now.

'Perhaps just a little more wine and conversation?' he said. 'I mean, we've only just met.'

Rachel felt as if she'd been slapped. One minute she thought he was about to kiss her, and then it was all off. She didn't know what to think. She took a sip of wine and looked at him. His dark eyes seemed to be deep pools but she couldn't guess what he was thinking, and he seemed to blow hot and cold so much it confused her.

He wound his fingers in hers and her heart started to beat quickly again. She stared at the shadow on his jawline and wanted to touch it, and then couldn't drag her eyes away from his lips . . . they were coming closer . . .

And then they were on hers and she closed her eyes. Suddenly she had the sensation of falling, like Alice in Wonderland falling down her rabbit hole. She almost lost her bearings of where she was or what was happening, except that it was dark and warm and stars were exploding like fireworks somewhere in her imagination and her whole body was tingling all over.

She'd been kissed before, but she'd never been kissed like this.

Grant's hand cupped her face and she could smell the honey and fresh spice of his cologne, but his kiss was like a chemical reaction, firing every particle she was made of, sending her senses haywire. Then suddenly she felt cold air on her face again as he pulled away.

'Sorry, I don't know what came over me,' he said awkwardly. 'I'm not in the habit of doing that in a public bar. Sorry.' He brushed off his sleeves and looked around, a little embarrassed.

But Rachel didn't want him to apologise. She didn't care if anyone was watching; all she wanted was for him to kiss her again.

4

Rachel closed the door to her flat behind her and heard the click of the Yale lock. She pressed her back against the cool door and took several deep breaths. Home; she was home. She put her handbag down in its usual place beside the hall cupboard.

She hadn't stayed long after . . . after that kiss. She'd been all flustered, as if she'd drunk too much and her brain had stopped working, and the conversation had gone so awkward. And so she'd made some pathetic excuse about being tired and just bolted.

The last time she'd gone for a spur of the moment drink with someone it had ended in a five-year relationship. A relationship, with hindsight, she may as well have not wasted her time with.

She'd assumed she was on the rosy path to marriage and a family but

Russell had another fish to fry; to be precise a rather pretty nurse with auburn hair called Angelina. She'd thought she'd coped very well with the break-up until six months later, when the news came through that Russell and Angelina had got engaged.

Six months! She'd waited patiently for five years for him to pop the question and it had never happened. And then, only a year later, she'd heard via a friend of a friend that they'd had a baby.

In a strange way, once she got over her initial envy, she was happy for them. In her heart of hearts, she knew Russell had never been The One.

Still, to have a baby, to have a family of your own, was something she knew she yearned for. She thought of her parents, who had now been dead for nearly ten years — and her only sibling, Becky, who had Jamie and was now expecting a baby.

She went into the kitchen and turned the kettle on.

It had been three years ago now since Russell had left her but she was still wary. She was happy to date, but slow to embark on anything that might be called a relationship.

But there was something about Grant Mackenzie that instantly sent her pulse racing and all her good sense flying straight out the window. It was like being at school again and having a crush.

Yes, that was exactly what it was; just a crush and she'd get over it.

She pulled the tea bags from the cupboard and took down a mug. The ritual of making tea made her feel a little more in control.

Grant Mackenzie was only a man. She'd known him for a very short space of time. He was smart and good-looking, any woman would be attracted to him. They had been out once and they'd kissed; that was all.

She tried to ignore the little voice inside her saying that wasn't all it was, that Grant Mackenzie was much more of a threat to her heart than she wanted to admit.

She heard the mundane ringtone of her mobile. She'd better answer it; you never knew. She fished the phone from her handbag. 'Hello?'

It was her sister Becky. She sounded very distressed, and it took a moment for Rachel to understand what the problem was. 'Try and stay calm and put your feet up. I'm coming right over.'

* * *

'It's probably nothing,' Rachel said straight away. Becky looked drained and anxious and Jamie wasn't helping by pacing up and down and frowning anxiously. Rachel sent him into the kitchen to make them a hot drink. 'Right, Sis, feet up on the sofa and try to relax.' Becky did as she was told. Rachel sat down in an armchair. 'When did it start?'

'A couple of hours ago. I did try and

call you on your mobile earlier, but I couldn't get an answer.'

'I'm really sorry, I didn't hear my phone.' She would have been in the bar with Grant. Another reason not to get involved with a man. 'Any pain?'

'No. You already asked me that.'

'Yes, I did. Sorry. Well a little spotting in itself means nothing and most likely your pregnancy is absolutely fine — '

'But it wasn't just a little,' Becky interrupted anxiously. 'And I looked it up on the internet and it said you should be checked out.'

So why not just head over to Granby General then? Rachel wanted to snap. *Why call me, half-way across the city, on my evening off . . . ?*

Rachel stopped her train of thought. She was being petty and ungracious and if she had been in Becky's shoes, she would have done exactly the same thing. 'Why don't we wait another hour and if you're still spotting, we'll go to the hospital to get checked out.'

'I don't like hospitals,' Becky muttered.

'Well, we could wait and see how you are in the morning?'

Becky looked away.

Jamie appeared right on cue with a pot of filter coffee and mugs on a tray. He put them down on the coffee table. Rachel would have preferred tea at this time of the evening, but she said nothing.

'What's the news?' he asked.

'Probably go to the hospital in an hour to get checked out. Unless . . . ' Becky put her head in her hands.

'Darling!' Jamie rushed to her side. 'I'm sure it'll be fine.' He wrapped his arms around her and Becky buried her head in his jumper. 'Rachel's here. How many expectant mums have an obstetrician for a sister?'

'Really I'm sure there is nothing to worry about.' Rachel felt a pang of jealousy at the couple's closeness. To have someone to share life with — its downs as well as its ups — was something she longed for.

'Easy for you to say,' Becky muttered.

51

Rachel bit her tongue. She could have been relaxing at home now. She'd probably be running a bath with an expensive sachet of bath salts. Her chance for some relaxation before another busy day tomorrow.

Her stomach growled. Actually, what time was it? She hadn't eaten since a quickly grabbed sandwich for lunch.

'Have you guys eaten yet?' Rachel kept her voice bright.

'No, we haven't.' Jamie raked his hand through his hair. 'Gosh, Becky, you should be keeping your strength up. Let me pour the coffees for starters.' He disentangled himself from Becky.

'Maybe we could send out for pizza?' Rachel suggested.

'I'm not hungry.' Becky shook her head.

'Well, I'm starving,' Jamie said. 'Pizza sounds great. There's a flyer from one we used a few times before in the kitchen, Rachel. Hang on a tick.'

'I might be losing my baby and all

you two can think about is pizza!' Becky burst into tears.

Rachel reached her just before Jamie did and enveloped her in a bear hug. 'I'm sorry, Sis. It's just that it's been a long day and I've not had anything since lunchtime. I really am starving.'

'Of course you are.' Becky sniffed. Jamie handed her a tissue. 'I'm being unreasonable . . . all these raging hormones . . . '

The pizza took ages to arrive and Rachel was about ready to eat the arms of the sofa. After there was nothing left except pizza boxes, Becky went into the bathroom. She and Jamie waited for her return in silence.

Becky wore a smile when she came back. 'Good news, I think. Nothing.'

'Well, I'd say there's little point in going to the hospital now,' Rachel smiled back. 'See how you feel tomorrow, but if it starts again and you're at all worried just go straight to the hospital.'

'Not to my GP?'

'They'll just refer you to the hospital

anyway.' Rachel stood up and picked up her handbag. It was getting late and she just wanted to be back in her own place. 'Well, see how you feel, but you might decide you'd like the reassurance of a scan anyway.'

'Are you going? Sorry, Sis. You know . . . '

'No need to say sorry, it's perfectly understandable for you to worry.' Rachel shook her head and hugged her sister goodbye.

★ ★ ★

A Cafe Alberto coffee was waiting for her on her desk the following morning. Rachel lifted the lid; black Americano, still hot. Perfect.

The office was empty but she guessed Bettina must have left it for her.

She liked Bettina, and it was more than just having a morning coffee service — she had asked some intelligent questions yesterday and Rachel had been impressed. She sat down and took a sip and wondered if she should send Bettina up to the Labour Ward today, or keep her with her.

Glancing at the clock, Rachel saw she had twenty minutes before Professor Larsson's clinic, so she had time to check her emails. There wasn't much that needed her attention, so she was able to reply to the few that did in just a few minutes.

As she did, she was aware of the door opening and called out, 'Thanks for the coffee.'

'Thanks for a great evening.' The slow burr sent her spine tingling. Grant!

Rachel spun around on her chair. 'What are you doing here?'

'This is your office, right?'

'Y-yes, of course.' What was it about this man that made her knees turn to jelly? She just about managed to keep him from dominating her every thought by keeping herself distracted with mundane things such as which of the choice of two cereals she should have for breakfast.

Now here he was, and she couldn't say she was disappointed. With his tall figure and broad shoulders, he filled the room with his manliness.

'You left rather abruptly last night. And I just wanted to say sorry.' He stepped closer. 'I shouldn't have, you know . . . kissed you like that.'

Yes, you should, Rachel thought. He stood beside her, so close they were practically touching, and she felt her heart beating in her throat.

'And I'm sorry I left so suddenly,' she said. 'It's just, it was late, I was tired . . . ' *I knew if you kissed me again that . . .* actually, she thought, she hadn't a clue and she'd been too scared to stick around and find out. There, at least she'd admitted as much, if only to herself.

He raised an eyebrow. Rachel knew her excuses sounded pathetic. 'So we might do it again, then . . . have a drink on a night we're less tired?'

'I'm always tired,' Rachel said despondently.

'So I was wondering, can I have your mobile number then?' Grant suddenly sounded very matter-of-fact and appeared to have ignored her comment. 'It'll save me from having to hunt you down in your office.'

Rachel smiled; she couldn't help smiling at his humour. But he wanted her mobile number — this was all sounding dangerously close to dating. But she merely said, 'Of course,' and gave him the number.

He took out his own mobile and tapped the number in. 'Thanks,' he said and then he snapped his phone shut.

Rachel expected that any moment now he'd ask her if she was free again this evening, or another evening soon, but he didn't. He merely turned on his heel and said, 'See you,' before he walked out of the door, nearly bumping into Bettina.

'Hi, Bettina.' Rachel wasn't sure whether she should be feeling cross or upset. She wanted to see him again, didn't she? Of course she did. Last night she'd just been running scared. But he'd just walked off with not a word that they might go out again. She took a long gulp of coffee.

At least he has your mobile number, a little voice said.

'Who was that?' Bettina asked. 'Oh, and call me Tina, if you like. Bettina's like my formal name and I've always hated it.'

'Grant Mackenzie, one of the midwives,' Rachel kept her voice matter-of-fact. 'Thanks for the coffee by the way, Tina.'

'No worries. Yeah, I've seen him about, but always in uniform before.'

Rachel suddenly realised that she hadn't even noticed Grant had been in civvies. Of course, he was working nights from tonight. *That's why he didn't ask you out, you twit!* she scolded herself and immediately felt better.

'Not the sort you'd think would go into midwifery,' Tina continued. 'But hey, everywhere is always chronically short of midwives so who I am I to judge?' Tina gave a smile. 'He's quite nice-looking, don't you think?'

'Sure,' Rachel said and pretended to look at her computer screen. 'Are you joining me for Dr Larsson's clinic this morning, Tina?'

'Yes, please,' she replied with her usual enthusiasm.

★ ★ ★

Grant headed swiftly through the hospital concourse towards the main entrance and Cafe Alberto. He wasn't about to start making a habit of coming in when he was supposed to be off. Besides, there were things he wanted to do today before he lost his days to his run of night shifts.

Starting with kissing Dr Rachel Booth soundly. The thought had come unbidden to his mind and he frowned, reminding himself that there were some things even more important than Dr Rachel Booth.

He caught a taxi and only ten minutes later was outside a tall office building, all metal and tinted glass. 'Grant Mackenzie here to see Dr Prosser,' he said to the smart receptionist.

'Mr Mackenzie, Dr Prosser is expecting you. Please take the lift on the right there up to the fourteenth floor.'

'Thank you.' But he already knew where he was going. They had two floors in this building now, after taking an additional one only a month ago to house the expanding payroll. Kate Prosser's office was well furnished but not over the top as befitted her status as chief executive of a charity.

'Grant! How lovely to see you.' Kate greeted him effusively with a hug and air kisses. She was clever, slim, in her forties and the kind of woman he might have considered dating if he hadn't started off this whole project that had turned his life around. 'How are you? I can't believe you haven't come to see us for a couple of weeks.'

'You try being a midwife in a short-staffed city maternity department. My shifts have been all over the place and I'm starting a run of night shifts tonight so that's next week written off. Thought I'd better come in today and see what's been happening.'

'Of course. Coffee?'

'Actually I'm okay for the moment.'

Kate looked at her watch. 'I called a team meeting for ten but we've had some really promising stuff happening on the fundraising side so let me take you through that so you're up to speed.'

'Great.' Grant sat down in one of the leather armchairs.

The news was good. The new fundraising manager had been busy, securing a major corporate donation as well as approaching the sign-off stage on a three-year grant from a trust.

'If we get this grant,' said Kate, 'and we should, then our base funding for the hospital build is pretty much in place.'

Grant felt a small flip of a thrill in his

chest. When his brother had died, he put as much money as he could muster into a trust in his name, the Dr Andrew Mackenzie Trust, and decided that it must be used for something worthwhile. And then he'd been to Tanzania and seen for himself exactly what he must do: build a hospital.

Two years later and he was sitting here at the headquarters of the charity that had been set up to administer the whole project, and it was looking as if his dream was now very close to becoming a reality. The money for the build was nearly there, and all they needed now was to work on the funding for the ongoing running costs.

'If you want something hard enough, it's yours,' their father had always said to them. He had been another Mackenzie who had gone before his time, dying of a heart attack at the age of only fifty-eight. Andrew had just taken up his first position as a Registrar and he'd had to throw it all in and return to Scotland to sort everything out.

Because you were too busy swanning about doing nothing useful, Grant's conscience told him. Yes, he could have decided to grow up then and become a responsible adult — rather than leaving it all on Andrew's shoulders and ruining his brother's promising medical career.

He could never make amends for that, he knew, but he could make a start by building this hospital that would make such a difference to so many people's lives.

'It's nearly ten now, Grant — let's go and meet the team,' Kate said.

'Sure thing.' Grant stood up and followed her to the door. 'But, Kate, you've not told me how you're keeping?'

Kate Prosser's marriage had broken up a year ago, after twenty years. Indeed, when she'd applied for the job she'd pretty much confessed that she needed something to work hard at to take her mind off everything.

'Fine, fine. Water under the bridge

now.' She waved a hand dismissively. 'Actually, I went out on a date last week which was actually very nice, and I'm seeing him again at the weekend.'

'Good for you,' Grant said and gave her a little squeeze on the arm.

'I expect people tell you all the time, but just in case they don't, you're a really nice human being, Grant.'

'I'm working on it, anyway,' Grant said awkwardly, scratching the back of his head like a schoolboy. 'Come on, then — lead me to the team.'

5

Her beeper went off. Rachel hastily gulped down the remains of her third cup of coffee. Was that old wives' tale of a full moon sending women into labour true? Her beeper had been going crazy since she'd started the night shift. It was only midnight and it was already turning into a long night.

'Labour Ward, Room Five,' a midwife at the station instructed her. Rachel glanced up at the white board but there was no information on it apart from the mother's name, and that looked Eastern European.

She hurried down the corridor, knocked on the door of Room Five and entered without waiting for a reply.

The mother looked young and exhausted. Rachel introduced herself but didn't get much of a reaction.

'No English,' said the student midwife

who was sitting with her.

Rachel quickly gathered from the notes that the mother had been on the labour ward nearly twenty-four hours now, but that labour was progressing very slowly, only one centimetre in the last three hours with no progress in the previous eight hours. Rachel checked the latest tracing from the baby monitor; it looked fine.

'Is there anyone with the mother?' Rachel asked the student midwife.

'No, that's why I thought I'd sit here for a bit.'

'That's good,' Rachel replied with a thin, tired smile. It looked like this one was headed for a C-section, but with no other immediate problems Rachel wasn't going to make that decision just yet. 'She had an examination only half an hour ago and there has been a little progress,' she continued, 'so I think we'll examine her again in an hour and see where we need to go from there. Don't let her eat anything in case we do have to go to theatre. Perhaps see if you can encourage her to move around a bit.'

'She's very tired,' the student midwife offered tentatively.

'Do your best,' Rachel said kindly and put the notes back.

While she was here, she might as well check on the diabetic mother in Room Two. She'd got to eight centimetres and wasn't far off the big event.

As it was, she was progressing nicely and, sure enough, within the next half hour gave birth without any intervention to a seven-pound baby boy whom the parents had already decided to name Christopher.

That was the best part of the job, Rachel thought. No matter how many times she saw new life come into the world, it was always a miracle to her.

As she went to wash her hands, she suddenly found herself thinking about Becky. She had gone to Granby General after the spotting scare after all, just to check everything was okay, and it had been. That was over two weeks ago now and Becky would have been in touch if she'd had any more problems, and yet still Rachel was inexplicably worried.

In fact, she just realised that it had also been over two weeks since she'd seen Grant Mackenzie and she'd heard nothing from him either. She'd thought she might, considering he had turned up in her office the next morning asking for her mobile number.

She bit her lip. It was a shame . . . she had liked him, liked him a lot.

But she didn't have time to think about that now. There was another mother waiting for her, another birth to supervise, followed, no doubt, by several others.

By the time her night shift finished at eight the next morning, she felt so tired that she was thankful she didn't drive into work, or she would be falling asleep at the wheel. This morning, however, even the fifteen-minute walk home seemed like a marathon.

She took deep lungfuls of the cold morning air and looked about her at the various people in the street going about their business: a baker arranging croissants in his shop window, a man in a leather jacket walking a dog, a teenage paper delivery boy with his bright orange trolley.

Her phone beeped. She fished it out of her handbag to see a text message had arrived: *R U free tonite? Becks xxx*

She found herself feeling unreasonably disappointed to see that it wasn't from Grant Mackenzie, but she texted a reply to Becky: *Sorry. On nights til Wed. R U well? Rach x*

First Grant had been doing a run of night shifts, and now her. A relationship between two people with such incompatible working hours would never work anyway; they'd never see each other.

Becky's reply appeared quickly: *I'm great thx. C U soon. B xxx*

Rachel put her mobile back in her bag. What was she doing even thinking about a serious relationship? She really must be tired.

As if on cue she stumbled on a jagged bit of paving stone and had to hold onto a lamppost to stop herself falling. *What an idiot!* she thought.

'Rachel? You all right?' It was a woman's voice.

Rachel looked up to see one of her neighbours, a woman she'd only met once before in the hall to her apartment block the day she'd moved in. The woman had been friendly and introduced herself, but Rachel couldn't for the life of her remember her name.

'It is Rachel, isn't it?' The woman frowned.

'Yes, Rachel Booth. I'm afraid I can't remember . . . '

'Kate Prosser. We live in the same apartment block.' The woman smiled.

'Yes, that I do remember.'

'Is your ankle okay? Can you put your weight on it?'

'It's fine, thank you.' Rachel put her foot down gingerly. 'Don't worry,' she added. 'I am a doctor.'

'Me too,' Kate Prosser said and

smiled in a relaxed kind of way that made Rachel feel at ease. 'Although I'm not practising any more.' Kate shook her head and added, 'I actually run a medical aid charity now.'

'How interesting. I've just started at City Hospital in maternity. I've just come off a night shift, actually.' Rachel found herself warming to Kate Prosser immediately.

'Ah, well, you'd better get home and to bed then. Perhaps we could get together for a drink sometime? Actually why don't you just pop over whenever you do have a free evening for a glass of wine? I'm in number thirty-nine. I'm usually around in the evenings.'

'That would be lovely.' Rachel wondered why such an attractive and educated woman as Kate didn't have a long term partner. It sounded as though she lived alone. But she decided that she definitely would pop over for that glass of wine.

★ ★ ★

It was Friday before Rachel felt near normal again. You never did night shifts for long enough to get used to them and so switching back to sleeping at night again wasn't too much of a problem, at least not for Rachel, although she always had a few days of lingering tiredness.

On Friday morning she forced herself out of bed early and went for a short swim at a local leisure centre she'd found out about that was handily just around the corner from the hospital. It was really good for a local pool; modern and clean, especially as she was only one of three people using it so early in the morning. She'd certainly go back.

She stopped at the drinks machine in the foyer and found some coins for a can of cola — a rare treat. The can was ice-cold, so she opened it straight away and took a long, grateful slug.

'Secret lemonade drinker, eh?' said a familiar male Scottish voice.

'Grant!' Rachel almost choked on her mouthful of cola. She quickly put her sleeve to her mouth, which only make it worse since the cola was sticky and likely to stain.

'Now if I were a proper gentleman I'd have a handkerchief but I've just been to the gym and I haven't. Sorry.'

'Don't apologise. I'm the clumsy one.' She tried not to think about him in the gym. He hadn't called her, and she was so over him and determined she was not about to go weak at the knees now.

'Are you going straight into the hospital?' He stared at her stained sleeve. Rachel nodded. 'Blot it with some washing-up liquid suds and then two parts water to one part vinegar.'

'Thank you. But where am I going to find vinegar in maternity?' She was more than a little surprised to find that Grant Mackenzie was an unexpected fountain of domestic knowledge.

'The hospital canteen?' He smiled.

He wouldn't get to her with that smile — he hadn't phoned and Rachel found herself feeling unaccountably cross.

'Come on, my car's just over there — I'll give you a lift.'

'Thanks,' Rachel said, despite her better judgment and the fact that they were only a few hundred yards from City Hospital.

'I've been doing nights, you've been doing nights . . . ' he said as they walked out of the leisure centre into the car park. So he'd been checking out her shifts then? 'The car's here,' he added, indicating with his hand.

Parked directly outside the leisure centre entrance, on an expensive parking meter, was a dark blue sports car. Rachel blinked as the side lights flashed on and off when Grant pointed a key in its direction — it was hardly the sort of car you expected a midwife to be driving. But then, Grant just wasn't your typical midwife in any way.

He opened the car door for her. 'I didn't see you in the gym . . . '

'No, I was swimming,' she replied. 'I'm not a gym bunny — I get enough of a workout at work.'

Grant snorted. 'True enough.'

Rachel slid into the soft leather-upholstered passenger seat. The dashboard was dark wood and chrome and the whole interior had a feel of luxury. If Grant Mackenzie had the money to buy this kind of a car, then what on earth was he doing working as a midwife?

'It's a shame we don't do more water births if you're into swimming.' Grant's voice cut into her train of thought.

'Very funny — not.' She buckled her seatbelt.

He got into the car and at once the confined space seemed to be overwhelmed by his maleness and Rachel wondered if this whole accepting a lift thing was a mistake. Perhaps she should walk after all? But he started the engine and then it was too late.

'I was fanatical about swimming when a teenager, with a cupboard full of trophies and all that,' she chatted on, trying to hide her awkwardness. 'They're still at my parents' house. It wasn't until University when the swimming finally had to take a back seat,' she rambled on. 'I couldn't fit in swimming training and do a medical degree.'

'That's a shame,' he replied, appearing to be genuinely interested. 'Everyone should have something they can pursue with passion.'

She wasn't sure if she was passionate about swimming any more. No, she'd definitely grown out of it. Indeed, what did she have in her life apart from her job, she wondered — Becky and a few University friends now scattered about the country?

'Tell me, when did you get to be so knowledgeable about household stains?' she said, changing the subject.

'We had an excellent butler when I was a boy. I used to spend a lot of time with him watching everything he had to do. I guess you just absorb stuff at that age.' He grinned. 'Although I've never actually tried to remove a cola stain with washing-up liquid and vinegar.'

His parents had a butler? Where did they live — Brideshead Revisited? She imagined Grant standing in the grounds of some great country house somewhere and wasn't sure if it suited him. She was lost for a reply and was grateful to find they had arrived when he turned into the hospital car park.

'Thanks for the lift,' she murmured.

'My pleasure.'

There was a short silence and Rachel wondered whether he might mention seeing her again, now they were back on day shifts. He drew into a parking space in one smooth move and switched off the engine.

Rachel decided to bite the bullet. 'You didn't call me,' she said.

'No.'

'I was a little surprised.'

'Things are a little complicated . . . '

'You mean you already have a girl-friend?' Rachel felt herself feeling cross again. 'Or a wife . . . ?'

'No, no, nothing like that.' He shook his head. 'Listen why don't we meet for coffee later at Cafe Alberto? Do you think you'll be able to take a few minutes off for lunch?'

'Probably not until about two.' She had a clinic this morning until one but it always seemed to overrun; Professor Larsson was very thorough.

'Okay, let's try anyway, and if you can't make it I'll call you later, I promise.' He sounded so sincere she hadn't the willpower to continue to hold a grudge against him.

They walked together into the main entrance and then went their separate ways, with Grant heading for the lifts and Rachel for her office which was on the ground floor.

Coffee in Cafe Alberto sounded very meagre compared to what she really wanted: a hot date. *Go on, admit it, you fancy Grant Mackenzie rotten*, she scolded herself. So much for getting over her crush.

Rachel walked into her office with a curious kind of spring in her step and tried to concentrate on the morning ahead.

Grant stepped into the lift and watched Dr Rachel Booth disappear out of view as the doors closed on her walking away from him. He wished he was on a beach somewhere, basking in the sunshine, or a nightclub with great music, or even in Scotland getting wet in the rain! Anywhere but the stifling confines of City Hospital with a long shift ahead of him.

Only another few months and he'd be out of here. If only he'd met Rachel on that beach or nightclub — anywhere in his old life — he'd not have thought twice about taking her out and all the rest. There was something about her presence that made him unsettled and he wasn't sure if he liked it. He had other things to do with his life now rather than chasing women.

Midday came around all too quickly. Grant took a few minutes' refuge behind the midwives' station. His stomach growled and he looked at his watch; half past twelve and he was supposed to be meeting Rachel at two. He sneaked into the pantry, but could only find a handful of custard cream biscuits in one of the tins. He had three.

Maybe he shouldn't meet her . . . actually, what was he meeting her for? They'd been on one date, If you could even call it that. He supposed he wanted to explain the circumstances as to why it would be a bad idea for them to take things any further. But one little kiss . . . One spur-of-the-moment kiss didn't entitle her to anything. And perhaps if he tried to explain it would just make things more complicated.

He helped himself to another biscuit from the tin and then he put the tin back in the cupboard and went over to stand by the window so he wouldn't snack any further.

The best course of action would be to meet her, that was only fair. But just keep it simple and say he wasn't interested but they could be friends. The usual patter. They were adults, after all.

Rachel threw herself down on the sofa the minute she walked back into her flat and threw a cushion onto the floor. Work-wise, it hadn't been a bad day. The clinic had gone well, she was getting the sense that the Prof was reasonably impressed with her, no real emergencies on the wards. But then meeting Grant in the morning and again in the coffee shop ... He'd dumped her soundly. Not that they had ever really been an item.

She got up, retrieved the cushion and stuck the kettle under the tap. Bother! She liked him and there was just no getting away from it.

And to top it all off, it was Friday night and she had nowhere to go and no one to see. Okay, so she was on duty over the weekend, but still ... she flicked the kettle on angrily.

Her neighbour, Kate Prosser, had said to come over for a drink. Probably Kate Prosser had a life and wouldn't be at home on a Friday night. Maybe, maybe not. The ritual of making tea calmed her down and she investigated the fridge for supper options. Not a lot, so she made do with some pasta and a jar of ready-made sauce.

She watched a few minutes of the news but there was not much of interest to her so she changed into something more comfortable, topped up her mascara and headed over to number thirty-nine.

As it was, Kate Prosser was at home. 'Come in, come in,' she invited cheerfully. 'You know this is perfect. It is Friday night after all and I've had a bottle of Sauvignon Blanc chilling in the fridge all day.'

Kate's flat was bigger than hers and with a better view. Rachel sank into a leather armchair and accepted a large glass of white wine. She wondered if she had bought or rented, but didn't like to ask.

'I hope you don't mind me being nosey right away,' Kate said, 'but I'm surprised you're not doing anything else on a Friday night. No boyfriend?'

'Actually, I'm on duty all weekend.' Rachel smiled. 'But no, there's no boyfriend either.'

Kate curled up on the sofa. 'It's been a really long week for me, including being away for a couple of nights at a conference. I always treat myself to a good bottle of wine for the weekend — and the weekend starts here.'

'Absolutely!' Rachel clinked glasses with Kate and she couldn't help warming to her neighbour. 'What does your charity do?'

'Actually, nothing yet, but we're planning and fundraising to build and run community hospitals in Africa where people are hours from any organised medical care. The first one will be in a very remote part of Tanzania.'

'That must be so worthwhile. I had thought about volunteering in Africa between school and University but then I didn't ever get round to it. I was just too young and too keen to get on with my studies, I suppose.'

'Well, I've been a corporate shark all my career up until now.' Kate took a long sip of wine. 'This is a bit of a departure for me, going into running a charity. But my life needed to change. I was married and it broke up.'

'I'm sorry to hear that.'

Kate shook her head. 'Oh, it was the usual thing . . . he went off with a younger woman.' Kate shrugged. 'Anyway, I won't bore you with all that. I'm really enjoying working for a charity. Tell me, what do you do at City Hospital?'

Rachel shared a little about how she was finding it so far; a busy but friendly department. Kate shared some tips on local shops and restaurants and then they got onto discussing music and found they both liked a number of the same artists.

When Kate went into the kitchen to refill their glasses Rachel glanced at her watch. She was surprised to see that well over an hour had passed! She didn't want to outstay her welcome.

Kate reemerged from the kitchen with the wine bottle.

'Just a small top-up for me,' Rachel said. 'Knowing my luck it will be a manic day tomorrow.'

'We should do this again,' Kate said.

'Yes I'd like that.'

'Actually there's a ball being organised for the charity next month. You know the type . . . posh hotel, dinner, dancing. Would you like to come?'

Rachel shook her head. 'Thanks but I wouldn't have anyone to bring.'

'Oh, you can join me on my table. I already have two of the trustees coming without partners so you'd be doing me real a favour in balancing the numbers out.'

'Go on then, put me down for a ticket,' Rachel replied rashly — but why not? She was a doctor and it was a medical charity, and it wasn't as if she had a packed social calendar. One evening with a nice meal and perhaps a bit of dancing with some people she'd never met before would give her a chance to relax and think about other things apart from the hospital.

And Grant, a little voice in her head added.

'Great, that's settled then,' Kate said. 'I'll email you the details.'

6

Rachel popped behind the midwives' station to put some patient notes back. No sooner had she done so than there was a bustle of frantic activity from down the corridor.

'Help!' A nurse came running down the corridor. 'We have a situation! A patient's stuck in the lift and she's in labour!'

'Coming!' Rachel checked her stethoscope was in her pocket and hastened off to the scene along with Amanda, an Australian midwife.

A couple of hospital cleaners had gathered outside the lift doors on the first floor and a technician was attempting to do something.

'What's happening?' Rachel asked the technician who had by now opened a box of wires in a panel next to the lift.

'It's stuck between the ground and

first floors. It's done this before. Half an hour tops and we'll have it sorted, love.'

'Those lifts should be condemned,' Amanda said as she caught her breath. 'Last year someone got stuck in one and had a heart attack. Now we're about to have our first lift birth.'

Rachel ran her fingers through her hair. She didn't see what they were going to be able to do. 'Can we speak to her — is the intercom working? Is there anyone in there with her?'

'Here.' The technician shoved a receiver into her hands and pressed a button. The cries of a woman in pain came through immediately.

'Hello?' Rachel said loudly. 'Can you hear me? I'm a doctor. Doctor Rachel Booth. Is there anyone in there with you?'

'It's all in hand, Dr Booth.' A familiar male voice crackled over the airwaves. 'This is Anna Brown,' he told her calmly. 'It's her third child and there are no complications, although baby's crowning now.'

'Okay, Anna, we'll get you out of there as soon as we can.' Rachel said, although she doubted the mother was even listening.

She leaned against the cool pillar beside the lifts and felt useless. Grant Mackenzie was in the lift, which was fantastic, but it did have to be Grant, didn't it? Of all the midwives in this hospital!

She'd been doing her best to avoid him over the last couple of weeks but suddenly her feelings came washing back. She bit her lip. She needed to stay calm and in control. Grant was just the midwife and she was just the doctor and it was nothing more complicated to it than that.

'Okay, the technician says it won't be long and you'll be out of there.' She switched the receiver off for a moment and turned to the technician. 'We haven't got half an hour — the baby is about to be born any minute. Do we call the fire brigade or what?'

'Fire brigade.' Amanda stood with

her hands on her hips. 'I'll go and get a bed and a bassinet.'

Another technician came running along the corridor towards them.

'The baby's about to be born,' Rachel said to him. 'Can you make sure the fire brigade get here quickly?'

'We can get the doors open,' he offered. 'Will that help?'

'Yes!' Rachel couldn't believe this was only just being mentioned now 'Of course that will help!'

Both technicians immediately set to work and managed to lever the doors open within minutes. There was about a two-foot gap; just enough to pass a baby through if necessary, although that didn't solve the problem of the mother should she develop post-birth complications.

Rachel got down on her knees on the cold floor and leaned in. The cry of a newborn baby pierced the air.

'He's got a fine pair of lungs,' Grant said and turned the newborn around to examine him quickly.

'A boy, is it?' Anna, the mother said.

'I never asked to find out.'

'Yes, and a good weight — seven or eight pounds, I'd say. Now shall I put him next to you on your chest for a bit?'

Grant had it all in hand and Rachel felt rather helpless watching. It was best the baby had a cuddle from his mother, since there didn't seem to be any other problems. Of course they still needed to cut the cord. Rachel came away and spoke to Amanda, who'd returned with a bassinet. 'Do you have something sterile to cut the cord?'

'Sure thing.' Amanda raced off.

The bed had also arrived, along with another couple of midwives and a hospital porter. One of the midwives Rachel didn't know — she might be agency staff — but the other was a Spanish midwife called Maria. Rachel had never warmed to her as she always seemed to be flirting with anyone male.

'Page Dr Holland please,' she told Maria. 'And make sure we have a delivery room ready.' Maria scurried off again.

Tina arrived eventually, too, but there was nothing either of them could do except pace up and down.

Rachel kept checking her watch. Ten minutes passed. The technicians were still scratching their heads and there was still no sign of the fire brigade. Rachel looked at Tina. 'Right, let's get the baby out so he can have his APGAR checks.'

Grant stood up and passed up the tiny infant, wrapped in a towel they'd passed down. It was lucky Grant was tall enough to do so.

Rachel caught his gaze for a heartbeat and thought she saw something in his eyes, something that spoke of a connection between them. And then she had the baby in her arms and the moment had passed and Grant was back attending to the mother, always the professional.

She passed the infant to Amanda who immediately put him into the special bassinet with its strong lights to keep him warm. Rachel got to her feet.

'Tina, stay here. I'll be back as soon as I'm satisfied the baby is okay.'

It didn't take long for Rachel to be sure all was well and she left the infant in capable hands. She arrived back at the lift to see firemen and that the doors had been opened and the mother was being lifted onto the bed. Rachel felt a huge wave of relief. They could get her to the delivery room and reunited with her baby again and check everything was as it should be. The mother certainly had a good colour in her cheeks.

'Ah, I seem to have missed the main drama.' Professor Larsson's dulcet tones echoed behind her. He acknowledged Rachel but made his way over to the bed. 'Professor Larsson, madam. We'll take you to your baby now. A bonnie lad, I hear. Dr Holland, perhaps you would like to join us?'

Tina nodded, no doubt pleased to have been singled out by the Prof. Rachel was sure that Professor Larsson was already thinking ahead to the public relations angle. He was a brilliant doctor but certainly that type. There was no medical argument why he should step in now and become involved in what would have been a very straightforward delivery were it not for the fact that it had taken place in a lift.

Grant stepped back from the scene to let others take over. He looked exhausted. Rachel felt tired too. Her part in this was also over now.

'You're such a hero, Grant.' Maria gave him a little punch on the upper arm. 'I bet she names the baby after you. They always do, you know.'

The crowd seemed to quickly melt away until it was only Rachel and Grant left standing there, as if they were lost.

'I'd better buy you a strong cup of tea with heaps of sugar,' Rachel said before she had time to think about it.

'Coffee,' Grant muttered and followed her to Cafe Alberto.

It felt slightly strange to be sitting facing him across the small table.

Rachel had fetched the drinks and also taken the liberty of buying two large muffins. 'Do you want the chocolate one or the low-fat blueberry one?'

'There's no point in low-fat muffins,' Grant said and leaned forward. 'And if you'd only admit it, you'll realise that you should have bought two chocolate muffins. You bought that blueberry excuse for a muffin for yourself but really you're secretly hoping I live for low-fat blueberry muffins so you can have the chocolate one that you should have bought for yourself in the first place.' He put his hands behind his head, leaned back and grinned.

Rachel smiled. 'You seem to know a lot about how women think. Do you have five sisters or something?'

'No.' His expression sobered but quickly brightened again. 'Handy for a midwife, though, don't you think?' He raised an eyebrow. 'Okay, I propose we cut both muffins in half and share, how does that sound?'

Rachel rested her chin in her hand.

'No, you have the chocolate one.'

'You know you don't mean that.' He got up and came back with a knife and divided the muffins. 'There you go.'

His half of the chocolate muffin disappeared in two bites, but Rachel savoured hers for a little longer. There was something special in sharing the muffins and she realised she was relaxed in his company for the first time since they had been out for that fateful drink. He was just a normal guy. Why she had ever got so stressed, she didn't know.

'So tell me, of all the midwives in this hospital how come you were the one who ended up in the lift?' she said.

'It's what comes from loitering around the main entrance. Actually I'd popped down during my break to post a letter. The mother staggered in, obviously in advanced labour, and was there a wheelchair to be seen?' Grant shook his head. 'I thought as she was still able to walk we'd get to the labour ward quicker than waiting for a porter to come up with a chair.' He shrugged his shoulders. 'I guess we should have waited.'

'It was a happy ending though, and you're bound to be in the papers.'

'That's true.' He fingered his chin. 'Maybe . . . ' He shook his head.

'What?'

'It doesn't matter.' He looked apologetic but Rachel had no idea why.

'Thank you anyway. You were marvellous in there — you did all the right things and without any real help.'

'Nonsense, you passed down a towel and a knife.' They both laughed.

Rachel met his gaze and her giggles subsided. Fate had brought them together again, she was sure. She enjoyed his company and she admitted that she still found him very attractive in a way that made her legs feel like jelly. She decided now was the time to be bold.

'Do you think we might go for that drink sometime? Perhaps tonight?'

But when he replied he spoke very

quietly and very slowly. 'No, Rachel, I don't think that would be a good idea.'

Rachel took a deep breath. 'Okay . . . I thought we had something in common, you know . . . I'm not asking for a relationship, just a date.'

'It wouldn't work,' he said. 'I have commitments outside work and, you know, work is pretty full on.'

'So you said.' Rachel took a mouthful of blueberry muffin, but it was dry and seemed difficult to swallow. She took a long sip of coffee. 'Well, you've made yourself perfectly clear. I'll not embarrass myself any longer.' She began to get up.

He placed his hand on her wrist which made her whole arm tingle and did nothing for her sanity. His voice was very quiet. 'Maybe I'm wrong, maybe you're right. I'd love to go out with you again, that's the truth of it.'

'Let's do it then.' Rachel found herself smiling. So she wasn't unattractive to him; it was just the 'commitments' in his life holding him back. She quelled the nagging doubt that the 'commitments' were actually a wife or girlfriend hidden away somewhere. Or a child? Maybe he had children. That she could handle, although why he couldn't just be upfront about it she didn't understand.

'Tonight then?' His lips twitched.

'Hmmm.' Rachel tossed her head back and tried to keep her voice light and steady. 'I might be washing my hair.'

'Not when I ask you out to my favourite Italian for supper.'

'I believe I was the one who asked you out,' she said teasingly. But just then another voice called over and interrupted the moment.

'Hey, Grant, hero of the hospital!' It was an older midwife Rachel didn't recognise. She stopped at their table.

'Linda, you're making me blush,' Grant said, although he didn't look at all like he was blushing.

'Did you hear, the mother is naming the baby after you?' Linda continued.

'She's calling him Mackenzie.'

'Well, at least the baby's a boy.' Grant tapped his fingers on his cup and Rachel got the sense that his smile was a little forced.

'See you later then, hero.' Linda raised her hand in a wave.

'See you, Linda.' Grant gave a nod and his colleague headed off towards the hospital main entrance.

'Mackenzie. It's not that unusual,' Rachel offered, feeling awkward now.

Grant put his head in his hands for a moment. 'I guess I'm just not looking forward to the bit where I have to speak to the newspapers.'

'I didn't have you down as the shy type,' Rachel said.

'It's not that, it's . . . well, I'm a male midwife and perhaps I have a bit of a hang up about it. I don't want to be noticed or singled out, I just want to get on with the job.' He stood up, pushing his chair back sharply so that it scraped against the floor noisily. 'I know someone has to report the news but they don't just do that, do they? They snoop and report on private lives.'

'Only if you're a celebrity,' she answered.

Grant shoved his hands in his pockets. 'Okay, better get back to it. Shall I come and pick you up later or shall we meet at the restaurant? The place I'm thinking of is Giovanni's, just off Park Street. Shall we say eight?'

Rachel quelled the disappointment that they wouldn't be getting together as soon as work finished. At least she would have a chance to go home and get changed. And Park Street was only a couple of streets from where she lived. She could probably walk there.

'Let's meet at the restaurant,' she suggested. 'I think it's pretty close to me in any case. It sounds nice, I'm looking forward to it.'

'Me too.' He gave her a smile that made Rachel's stomach do a back flip. She took a deep breath as he waved and headed off. She watched his tall frame with its easy gait until he was out of sight.

Perhaps he was just a very private individual and not happy with the prospect of being all over the newspapers, but it did make Rachel wonder if there was something more to it than that.

* * *

Giovanni's was a traditional Italian restaurant with rustic tables, pink tablecloths and fairy-lights in the half-misted windows. From the aroma that hit Rachel as she walked in the door she knew she was about to enjoy some delicious home-cooked food.

Grant was already there, enjoying a beer at the small bar. He spontaneously embraced her when she arrived and Rachel felt suddenly warm all over, even though it wasn't that warm in the restaurant. She shrugged her coat off.

'What would you like to drink?' he asked.

'Gin and tonic, please,' Rachel said and the waiter behind the bar immediately started to prepare it for her.

It had been such a long time since

she'd had a G&T she couldn't remember — they were for when you didn't have a care in the world, not for busy maternity doctors who hardly even had time for a life.

But tonight she was determined to be just Rachel, not Dr Booth, and Grant would be just Grant, not someone she worked with.

However, she couldn't resist opening their conversation with, 'Did the newspapers eventually catch up with you?

'Yes.' Grant grimaced. 'I have to say I'm not really looking forward to tomorrow's headlines.' He touched her hand and a shiver ran right up her arm. 'But let's not think about that tonight.'

'Of course.' Rachel took a sip of her G&T.

The maître d' came over, menus tucked under his arm. 'Your table, sir?'

'Thank you.' Grant hovered behind her as they made their way to their table, so close she thought that at any moment they'd be touching, but somehow she reached her seat without it happening.

The maître d' pulled out the chair for her, laid her napkin on her lap and handed her the menu. A lovely restaurant, a proper date . . . what more could a girl want? She smiled at Grant across the small table but he was already perusing the menu, so Rachel busied herself for the next few minutes deciding what dishes she was going to have. But once they had ordered Grant was Mr Attentive.

They talked about so many things, pausing as the main courses arrived. During the course of the conversation, Rachel realised that Grant knew all about her fairly ordinary suburban childhood but she knew almost nothing about his — apart from that curious remark from before about having a butler.

'Where did you grow up?' she asked.

'Scotland — can't you tell from the accent?'

'Scotland's a big place,' she said, trying to encourage him to talk more.

'Oh, in the middle of nowhere.' He

tucked into his ravioli.

'I've only ever been to Edinburgh,' she persisted.

'I'd never been abroad until I was sixteen. My father didn't do abroad, although he did once take us to London to look around the Natural History Museum and visit his tailor.'

Visit his tailor? Add that to the butler he'd mentioned and Grant must come from a very well to-do family. She couldn't help staring at him.

'Don't look so surprised,' he added. 'Anyway I made up for it later, when I went all over Europe during my 'wild' phase. I'm clearly over that now, as you can tell.' He gave her a winning smile and Rachel felt too warm again.

What did his background really matter? After all, he didn't come across as posh or stuck-up.

The meal seemed to be finished far too quickly. Rachel sipped her coffee as slowly as she could but it had gone cold long ago. She didn't want the evening to end, yet ending it was.

Grant asked for the bill. She let him pay it — she'd pick up the tab next time. If he was just on a midwife's salary, he couldn't keep taking her to places like this. If there was to be a next time . . .

'Shall I run you home? I've only had one small beer.'

'Thank you.' She just wanted to be in his company as long as she could.

They reached the front door to her flats all too quickly. He leaned over toward her in the passenger seat and gave her a peck on the cheek. A feather-like touch, over in an instant.

'Rachel, I like you a lot. It would be nice to do that again sometime.'

'Yes, yes of course. And on me, next time.'

He waved his hand dismissively.

She got out of the car reluctantly. He hadn't offered to walk her to the door. If he had, she would definitely invite him in for a coffee, but he didn't. He waited in the car while she fumbled with the keys to let herself in, to check she got in safely she supposed.

Once she was inside and on the other side of the door, she suddenly realised she was trembling.

A peck on the cheek — was that it? And a vague promise that they might get together again? Hardly the most promising of endings to the evening.

She been hoping for another kiss like that first one; a kiss that made her bones feel as if they were melting, as if she were being wrapped in velvet and cherished.

She threw her handbag down in its usual place and went off to bed in a distinctly bad mood.

7

Rachel stared and stared in utter disbelief at the black ink headline, big and bold across the front page of the Morning Express, and beneath it the sub-heading which read, *THANK YOU, M'LORD! ARISTOCRAT DELIVERS BABY IN HOSPITAL LIFT*.

'Are you buying that newspaper, love, or waiting for it to buy itself?' The newsstand vendor brought her back down to earth. Rachel fished about in her purse for some coins and took the paper across the road to a chain coffee shop where she could read it at her leisure.

Grant Mackenzie doesn't use his aristocratic title at work. 'It's not relevant,' he said. Indeed 'Duke of Bowness and Laird of Colquair' might be a bit much to fit on his NHS name badge.

Rachel shook her head and put the

paper down so she could drink the small coffee she'd bought. Questions kept running through her mind. Why had he said nothing to her last night? Surely he must have known that it would come out in the newspapers? Perhaps that's why he'd not wanted to talk about it, but he might have told her, especially if she was going to find out anyway.

She couldn't help feeling that this was yet more proof that she meant nothing to him.

She finished her coffee as quickly as she could or she would be late for work. That Grant was an aristocrat she could believe, now that she thought about it more. It certainly explained why he drove a fancy car and thought nothing of paying for dinner at an expensive and exclusive restaurant.

But the biggest question of all occurred to her as she arrived at the hospital's main entrance — what was the Duke of wherever doing working here as a midwife?

As soon as she reached her office — thankfully empty — she pulled the paper out again and reread the whole article. No, the Morning Express said nothing on the subject.

She typed 'Duke of Bowness' into a search engine on her computer. Colquair was a large estate and apparently the 'family home' of the Dukes of Bowness. Not this Duke, anyway.

The Colquair estate had its own website, all very upmarket. The house was open to the public in the summer and was also available for private hire as a corporate shooting venue. It also brewed its own 'Colquair' ale.

She found plenty more information about the historic Dukedom of Bowness but nothing on the present incumbent, apart from one tantalising sentence on a website about the British aristocracy, *Following the death of Andrew Mackenzie, the Dukedom passed to his younger brother, Grant*.

She sat back in her chair. Grant was a Duke who owned this huge estate in

Scotland — and yet he was living in England and working in an NHS hospital as a midwife.

There was only one conclusion: Grant had to be completely insane.

Her phone beeped. It was a text message from the mad male midwife himself. *I can explain. On ward. Coffee later? Grant*

She typed a quick text back before she could think better of it: *OK*.

But it wasn't okay. She didn't feel okay. She still felt hurt that he'd said nothing last night and she couldn't see how he was going to explain. She had no idea what she was going to say to him. She wasn't even sure she wanted to say anything. Perhaps it was just time to let this whole thing go.

This was exactly why she didn't do relationships, she reminded herself. She didn't want explanations and apologies. He should have been up front with her from the start.

She was on the wards this morning and she didn't have any clinics today

111

until the afternoon, so they were bound to bump into each other. Rachel just wanted to get on with her job. Another reason why going out with a work colleague was such a very bad idea.

★ ★ ★

According to the rota Rachel was supposed to be on the ward this morning, too, but Grant couldn't find her anywhere. He skulked behind the midwives' station for as long as he could get away with — its central position meant she'd have to pass by to get from the labour ward to antenatal and postnatal. But he had a feeling he must have missed her when he had to go and do some observations in antenatal.

He sunk back into a chair behind the midwives' station. The clock said it was nearly eleven. She would have read the newspapers by now and . . . well, half of him didn't know why he cared so much, but he felt guilty for not telling her last night.

She had every right to be cross with him and the truth was, he did want to see her again. Since he'd first laid eyes on Dr Rachel Booth, he'd not been able to get her out of his mind. There was something about her that was special. It had come to him last night as they'd enjoyed their meal and it had taken every ounce of his willpower to stay sitting in his car and leave her with the tiniest peck on the cheek, when what he'd really wanted to do was to kiss her passionately.

But whatever happened, she deserved better than this.

'Hey, Duke Mackenzie!' Maria came through the double doors.

'Hi, Maria.' Great, this was all he needed. Most of his colleagues had been kind enough not to bring up the newspaper revelations to his face although he was sure they'd all be talking about it among themselves.

'I always knew you were a dark horse.' Maria leaned on the midwives' station counter and fiddled with a strand of hair. 'But a Duke! Now that is truly impressive.'

Grant sprang to his feet as an anxious-looking couple came through the double doors, keen to put some distance between himself and the Spanish midwife. 'Can I help you?' he asked the couple.

'My wife's in labour,' the man flustered. 'We phoned earlier and they said just to come in.'

Grant blinked. The woman didn't even look pregnant. She was wearing several layers of clothes, though.

She suddenly let out a groan and panted. 'The contractions, they're coming really quickly now. Every two minutes or so . . .'

'What's your name?' Grant asked, getting out the registry forms.

'Stephanie Hobbs,' her partner answered for her.

Grant took the details and asked them to take a seat while he checked whether he could admit them to the labour ward.

'Please, hurry!' Stephanie called after him. 'You've got to do something. It's too soon for the baby to be born yet.'

'How many weeks are you?' Grant asked, concerned now.

'Twenty-six,' said her husband.

'Maria, page Dr Larsson.' Grant ran into the labour ward to find the most senior midwife he could. He'd been in such a funk about Rachel and the newspapers. He should have noticed the woman didn't look anywhere like nine months. *Get a grip, Grant*, he admonished himself.

Distracted, he ran straight into Rachel.

'In a hurry to see me?' Rachel smiled.

'A woman, only twenty-six weeks, just come in.' Grant tried to catch his breath. 'Looks like she's in labour.'

Rachel swung into action instinctively and Grant seemed to be on autopilot. He got Stephanie into a bed, found extra pillows, and a chair for her husband. Rachel seemed to be an oasis of calm, Grant thought, always the professional — she really was an excellent doctor.

'Don't worry,' she said to Stephanie. 'We're going to give you some drugs that are very effective at stopping labour. We'll also give you a steroid injection to strengthen the baby's lungs.'

Grant went off to find a baby monitoring machine to do a trace. He chewed his lip. He couldn't imagine what the parents were feeling. He couldn't remember the odds of a pre-term surviving at twenty-six weeks but they were dicey. Thirty weeks was the number to try and reach, but every extra week you could hang on, the baby's prospects improved.

He found a trace machine at last — people were always wheeling them off and then forgetting to put them back.

Stephanie seemed a lot calmer when he returned and once he'd set up the monitor, the contractions coming through weren't as strong as he feared.

Rachel came back into the room and consulted the trace. 'How are you feeling?' she asked the mother.

'Better, I think. And I'm not sure if I'm still having contractions. Will the drugs be working already?'

'I hope so. Now it's really important

that you try to relax as much as you can. I'll come back in twenty minutes and see how you're doing, but in any case you're going to be on bed rest for the rest of this pregnancy.'

'Does that mean I have to stay in hospital?'

'We'll have a chat about it when I come back.'

Grant followed Rachel out of the room. 'What do you think, doc?'

'It looks okay but let's wait and see. I think we definitely need to keep her in overnight in any case, so could you book her in to antenatal?'

Grant gave a mock salute and Rachel gave him a slightly shy smile. Now was his chance . . . 'Could I have a word?' He pushed open the door to the pantry, which was thankfully empty.

The pantry was a small rectangular room for use by the hospital catering staff, but they were only in evidence around mealtimes. It was out of bounds to patients and the midwives had a kitchenette in their rest-room. It was the one place on the busy maternity ward you might get some privacy.

Rachel leaned against the industrial dishwasher. She pushed her hair back and her eyes seemed to be sparkling. 'I've never dated a Duke before. That sort of thing doesn't usually happen to ordinary girls like me.'

'It shouldn't matter.' Grant spoke as if he had a shard of glass between his teeth. He exhaled deeply to force himself to relax. She was teasing him and he deserved it. 'I was never supposed to be the title holder anyway.'

'I'm sorry about your brother.' Rachel was staring at the floor.

'Yes, well, it was a while ago now. Anyway, by rights you should be bowing and scraping and calling me 'your Grace'.'

'By rights I should be having you committed to a mental asylum. I can't believe how flippant you are about the whole thing.'

'I never asked to be a Duke. But I do want to apologise, for not telling you. It wasn't fair to leave you to read all about it in the newspapers. I should have thought. I'm just in denial about it most of the time.'

'I can see that. Now maybe you can tell me something else — what the Duke of Bowness is doing working here at City Hospital as a midwife?'

'It was quicker than becoming a doctor.'

'So you were going to become a doctor but then you decided no, you'd become a midwife because it takes less time to qualify?' Rachel asked incredulously, her eyes wide.

'Basically, yes.'

She exhaled sharply in disbelief. 'You really are mad.'

'Rachel . . . wait.' He clasped his hand over her hand on the door handle. She stopped in her tracks and the air seemed to electrify between them. He moved even closer so his chest enveloped her back and she was perfectly placed for his lips to brush the back of her neck in a feather-light kiss. He couldn't resist. He breathed in her fresh, citrus scent.

When she turned around, her eyes were blazing. He thought she might shout at him and he took a step back.

Instead she threw herself into his arms and then he had her pressed up against the back of the door as he kissed her hungrily, her lips, her neck, wanting to drink in every inch of her. She was driving him crazy.

'Wait!' Rachel ducked away. She sounded breathless. His chest was pounding. 'This isn't . . . this isn't happening. I like you, but I can't . . . '

'You more than like me.' His voice came out like a growl.

'Okay, yes, but this isn't going anywhere. You're a Duke! You're . . . mad.'

'That has nothing to do with this. This is about you, not me. Problems with a past boyfriend?' Grant felt himself beginning to get angry. Who did Dr Rachel Booth think she was? She had been enjoying their kiss as much as he had, but now — again — she was pulling away.

'Look, it's just not going to work.'

'Why not let time be the judge of that?' Not that they had much time. Three months from now, he'd be hundreds of miles from here — under the blazing skies of Africa.

'I have to go.' She brushed down her shirt with her hands and straightened it, but she couldn't remove the flush from her cheeks. That gave him a certain feeling of satisfaction.

Reluctantly he backed away. 'This isn't the end of this.'

She didn't reply, but looked at him with a puzzled expression and he couldn't tell what she was thinking. He watched as she gingerly opened the door and escaped into the corridor.

He slammed a hand down on the worktop. It sounded like a cliché but he really had never felt like this about a woman before.

He had three months. Three months to win her around. And he really didn't want it to take that long.

8

Becky reached out and touched one of the white roses in the vase on Rachel's coffee table. 'Those are lovely flowers,' she said admiringly. 'Did you buy them yourself?' she added wryly. 'Or do you have an admirer you haven't told me about?'

'Are you going to decide what you want to eat?' Rachel waved the take-away menu at her and wished she'd thrown the flowers away now.

But they were lovely. Grant had sent her a bouquet every week for the last three weeks. First yellow roses, then pink, and now white. He was persistent, she'd give him that — and being sent flowers did tend to melt your heart a little bit.

But not enough. He just wasn't for her, he was just too complicated and she had enough stress at work. Outside work, she needed a simple life, not a Duke who wanted to be a midwife instead.

'Pizza I think, if that's okay with you.' Becky spoke and broke into her thoughts. 'I could eat an entire twelve-inch pizza with all the toppings, but I'll settle for a supreme with extra cheese.'

Rachel phoned through their order. Jamie had gone away overnight on business and so Becky had suggested she come and stay over. 'It's so nice having my sister in the same city,' she said.

'Yes it is,' Rachel agreed. She'd been thrilled when she'd seen the registrar's job at City Hospital advertised and even more thrilled when she'd got the job, because it had allowed her to move back and be closer to Becky. The last few years she'd not seen as much of her sister as she'd liked. They still had some catching up to do.

'Clearly there's nothing wrong with your appetite,' Rachel told Becky. 'But have you been keeping well?'

'Yes, yes — and no, before you ask, I've not been overdoing it. Oh, I had my twenty week scan last week . . . ' Becky fished in her handbag and pulled out a small envelope. 'Here are the pictures.'

Rachel looked through the grainy black and white images but she'd seen so many scan pictures, it was difficult to think that this would soon be her niece or nephew. 'Ah, so is it a boy or a girl?'

'We decided not to ask in the end so it will be a surprise on the big day. I don't mind either way. Anyway, enough about me.' Becky pulled her legs up onto the sofa and shifted herself around until she was comfortable. 'You've been quiet — too quiet.' She tapped her nose with one finger. 'Which means there must be something happening on the man front . . . '

'That and the roses on my coffee table you mean?'

'You didn't really buy them for yourself, did you?'

'Nothing to tell. They're from a man, yes, but there's nothing going on.'

'Ooh, a man has sent my sister flowers. Well, it's a start. Are you going to go out with him then? Who is it? Someone you work with?'

'We went out a couple of times but it didn't work out.'

'Why? I mean, you've not had those flowers long. He must be still keen.'

'He's daft as a brush.' Rachel shook her head. 'I have no idea how his mind works, but I do know he's just not right for me.'

'You have to go out with him again before you finally decide.'

'I don't think so.'

'I am the voice of wisdom.' Becky spoke in a deep, comedy voice. 'Do as I say.' She went back to her normal voice. 'Seriously, Sis, I bet he's good-looking, and rich and all those things normal girls less contrary than you actually find attractive.'

Rachel couldn't keep a smile off her face. 'Yes, he is good-looking actually

— and rich, and I work with him. You're some kind of mind reader.'

'No, just your sister, but I do know you. I remember every time there was a new pop sensation everyone liked, you always had to go against the grain and a find a reason why you didn't like them; wrong haircut or something. You're too picky, that's what you are. Whereas me, I was never looking for Mr Perfect when I met Jamie or he'd have fallen at the first hurdle.'

'Okay, I take your point.'

'Right.' Becky plumped up another cushion for herself, a self-satisfied smile on her face. 'Well then, send mystery man a text and get yourself another date with him.'

'Now?' Rachel gasped. 'But I've not really spoken to him for three weeks. It's not just that simple, you know.'

'You haven't thanked him for the flowers yet? Shocking!'

'I'll thank him for the flowers then, if only to keep you happy, but we'll wait and see about anything else, okay?'

'Well, okay for now, I suppose.'

Rachel got her phone out a little reluctantly. But Becky was right in some ways and if she admitted it to herself she still liked Grant — and it was mean of her not to have thanked him for the flowers. Any of the flowers.

'What shall I write?' Rachel's finger hovered over her phone keypad.

'Thanks for the flowers. They were lovely.'

Rachel typed. *Thx 4 flowers. All the flowers. They were lovely.*

'Aren't you going to sign it with a kiss?'

'No.' Rachel pressed send quickly, before she could change her mind. 'There, it's gone.' She put her phone down on the table and ran her hand through her hair. Would Grant text back? What would he say?

Her phone remained stubbornly silent.

He must be busy, she consoled herself. Perhaps he was at work at the hospital. But perhaps he didn't want to hear from her at all. But then again, if that was the case, why would he send her all those flowers? She topped up her glass of wine to try to distract herself from her own confused thoughts.

'Pizza should be here soon,' Becky said. 'I know what people mean now about eating for two, Rach. Honestly, if I don't eat for a couple of hours I'm absolutely starving.'

'Well I think I'll just nip to the loo.' Rachel bit her lip. *He must be busy*, she told herself firmly. 'Do you want anything from the kitchen?'

'No, I'm great thanks, Sis.' Becky waved at her still mostly un-drunk glass of orange juice.

'Are you drinking enough? You know when you're pregnant, you need — '

'Oh, stop fussing. I'm fine.'

Rachel heard the doorbell from the bathroom. Becky would answer it but what if she didn't have money for the pizza? She went into her bedroom where she always kept a couple of notes in a special sock in her sock drawer, just in case. She grabbed the sock. 'Coming!' she called.

Grant Mackenzie was standing in her living room.

'Hi, Rachel,' he said. 'And hi, Rachel's sock.'

'Oh,' she said. 'I thought you were the pizza delivery man.'

'Ah, I see. It's *his* sock, then.'

'No!' It was one half of a pair of novelty socks someone must have given her for Christmas years ago, and she'd long since lost the other half. Gosh, she was making a right meal of this. She thrust the sock down on the coffee table. 'Thanks for stopping by. Great to see you. Would you like a drink?'

Grant scratched the back of his head — a gesture she found incredibly endearing, much to her frustration. 'I might stay and steal a slice of pizza.'

'Oh, do,' Becky said. 'I like you already. Do you work with Rachel?'

'Yes.' Grant sat down and crossed his long legs at the ankles. He was wearing a very smart suit. Rachel wondered if he'd received her text. He must have, and then just decided he'd come over. She should be flattered, but the truth was she felt a bit out of her depth.

She wished Becky wasn't here. She wished Grant wasn't here. She had no idea what was on Grant's mind. She needed to chill and just run with it.

'Sure you wouldn't like a glass of wine or something?' she asked.

'Go on, then,' Grant said. 'A small glass would be great.'

'I'll get it.' Becky was halfway to the kitchen before Rachel even had a chance to reply.

Grant was looking at the roses on the table but he didn't say anything.

'I take it you haven't come straight from the hospital?' Rachel said.

'No, I was on my way out actually, but then I got your text.' He smiled. 'And as I was less than five minutes away and running early, I thought I'd just drop by in person.'

So he was on his way out somewhere else. Rachel took a deep breath and tried not to assume it was another woman. After all, he had got her text and he wouldn't have come here unless he was still interested, would he? She was tired, though, and not sure she fully trusted in her own logic.

'You don't mind, do you?' he asked, suddenly unsure.

'Of course not.' Rachel sat down quickly. 'I guess we have just been ships passing in the night these last couple of weeks.'

'Indeed.' Grant gave her a strange look. It all felt so awkward between them but Rachel wasn't sure what to do about it. Perhaps she should take the initiative. 'Are you doing anything on Friday night?'

'I'm afraid so.' He frowned apologetically.

'Saturday I'm at an old friend's wedding. I have to leave pretty early to get there — it's in Somerset.' Rachel waited to see if he suggested they might get together on Sunday or even suggest that his Friday night commitment

131

might be something he could get out of.

'I'm sure you'll enjoy the wedding,' was all he said.

Becky returned from the kitchen and handed Grant his glass of wine. 'Is that Catherine's wedding you're talking about — your old school friend?'

'Yes,' Rachel said. 'It's this Saturday.'

'Are you going with Rachel?' Becky asked Grant. Rachel could hardly believe her sister had the nerve.

'I'm on duty this weekend,' Grant said. He took a measured sip of wine.

Rachel let out a long breath. That was why he'd not said anything about them getting together over the weekend. She took a swig of her own wine.

'Rachel didn't mention you were expecting,' Grant said to Becky.

'I'm twenty-three weeks tomorrow.' Becks gave a huge smile. 'I'm amazed how quickly the time seems to be passing.'

'Are you having the baby at City Hospital?'

'You know, I wish I was, but because we live right over the other side of the city I'm registered at Granby General. Jamie — that's my partner — figured it made more sense, as any problems with traffic should be much less.'

Grant murmured something about traffic jams and took a long glug of wine while Becky started to talk about her nursery shopping plans.

Rachel was delighted for Becky about the baby, she really was, but Grant was here in her flat as her guest, and just because he was a midwife didn't make him an expert on baby equipment.

'Yes, you certainly want teething rails on the cot,' Grant said. He looked at Rachel with a trace of apology in his eyes. 'My cousin had two babies, they're four and six now.'

'I see.' Rachel bit her tongue. She didn't mean to sound frosty. 'What are their names?'

'Alice and Callum.' Grant took another sip of wine while watching her closely. Rachel wasn't sure she liked the scrutiny. Oh, why was this so difficult and complicated? If only Becky wasn't here. If only . . .

'Well, I had better be going, I'm afraid. I was supposed to be somewhere else ten minutes ago.' Grant polished off his glass and rose to his feet.

'Right, well . . . thanks for dropping by . . . nice to see you.'

Rachel wanted to kick herself in the shins — hard. She was treating him like nothing more than an acquaintance.

'Have fun,' Becky chirped.

Grant smiled at her. 'I'll try. It's a fundraising evening for charity . . . Actually, I don't suppose you girls would like to come along?'

'Sorry, we've got pizza arriving and a night-in planned.' Rachel went over to the front door to open it for him.

'What did you say that for?' Becky said the moment Grant had gone. 'We could have gone. He's nice, and he likes you. What's the problem?'

'I'm too tired to think about going out.' Rachel tidied Grant's empty glass away. She wasn't going to be drawn into a discussion with her sister about Grant. She really wasn't in the mood for that.

She would have probably agreed to go with him if Becky hadn't been here, but now he'd gone and she didn't know when, or even if, she'd be seeing him again.

★ ★ ★

The sun shone and the bride looked radiant but Rachel didn't really enjoy her friend Catherine's wedding. Everyone seemed to be in couples and every moment seemed to be designed to remind her that she wasn't about to marry anyone any time soon. Nor did she have anyone to dance with later after the wedding breakfast when the slow songs came on.

With all the travel it was a tiring weekend, and she was back at work on Monday and busier than ever as Dr Larsson was away at another conference. She came home on Monday evening to discover a plain envelope with her name on it had been pushed under the door to her flat. She picked it up. Her heart began to race with excitement. It was unsealed and she pulled the contents out — a small folded note enclosing a stiff cardboard ticket.

See you there on Friday. Kate

The ball, of course! She'd agreed to go, and why not? Should she pay for the ticket? Rachel turned it over but there was no mention of a price. The champagne reception was at six-thirty, though. That might be a bit of a push to get to in time from work. Dr Larsson should be back by then, however and, after all, it was a medical charity. She'd see if she could slip away half an hour early.

She put the ticket down on the side.

Of course she had hoped it was a message from Grant. She'd been checking her phone messages all weekend hoping for a text from him, but there was nothing. He'd sent her flowers and then he'd turned up at her flat. But then silence again and now she simply didn't know how things stood.

Maybe she should try and contact him? He was probably just busy, and tired if he'd been working the weekend — or even enjoying a couple of days off. She should have checked to see when he was working this week.

She went into the kitchen to prepare supper. Should she text him? Probably not. However much she might want to see him and hear from him, the ball was in his court.

She opened the fridge. Empty. Hardly surprising as she'd not had time to go shopping. She'd better pop down to the supermarket now, unless she wanted beans on toast with no toast.

She'd really had enough of thinking about Grant Mackenzie for now, she really had.

★ ★ ★

Grant stepped off the airplane at Aberdeen airport to be hit by a biting

North Sea wind. He got a lungful of cold air and pulled his collar up around his neck. With only hand luggage, he was through the terminal building in minutes and at the taxi rank.

His mobile beeped. He drew it out of his pocket to see he had a text message. From Rachel? No, just from his cousin Sandra asking him if he'd had a good flight and to call her later.

His thumb hovered over the keypad and for a moment he considered sending Rachel a text. She would have been busy over the weekend at her friend's wedding but she'd be back at work now.

He wondered whether she ever thought about him. She liked him, he knew that, but every time he had the urge to try and start something up with her, he had a pull in the other direction telling him it was better for them all that he didn't get involved. He was going to Africa in seven weeks. His life wasn't his own any more, just to follow every whim and fancy. He needed to remember that.

He put his phone back in his pocket.

He got into a cab and instructed the driver to take him to the city's general hospital. He stared out of the taxi's window at the granite buildings which seemed faintly hostile in the darkening sky. This was no longer a place of happy memories. And especially not this city, and this hospital, where Andrew had died.

His mother was in a side room that felt as stifling as a sauna, although she was sitting under the bed clothes and wearing a plush bed-jacket. She was even wearing make-up, but it didn't disguise how thin and frail she was.

'Grant!' She held her arms out and they embraced.

'Why didn't you tell me you'd had another turn?' he said. 'Why did I have to hear it from Cousin Sandra?'

'I didn't want to worry you, silly boy. You're always so busy down there in London. Have you had to take time off work?'

'No,' he lied. Well, it wasn't a

complete lie, since he had been able to just swap some shifts.

'Well now you're here would you pass me my knitting bag, dear. Someone put it in the locker and I can't reach it.'

Grant bit his tongue and fished in the locker and found a squashy patchwork bag that was a likely suspect.

'That's it, dear. I've started knitting for the little one.'

Grant placed the bag on her knees and his mother drew out a pair of knitting needles with a lemon-yellow work in progress on them.

'Neutral colours of course, as we don't know if it's a going to be a girl or a boy, do we?' His mother looked smug.

'Whose is this baby?' Grant didn't really care but it was conversation.

What he really wanted to do was speak to the doctor and see how serious things were. When Cousin Sandra had called and said his mother had had another heart attack, he could think of nothing else but getting here as quickly as he could. Now he was here, he hardly knew what he could do.

'Yours, of course, silly boy.'

'Mother . . . wouldn't I have to have a wife first?'

'There is that, but I just had this funny feeling, you see, and thought I should make a start.' She began to knit, her thin fingers quickly getting into the rhythm, clickety-click.

'Believe me, mother, when I do anticipate this happy event, you will be one of the first to know.' Grant felt his sinews tighten.

'Just call it a mother's intuition.' Clickety-click. 'You've been awfully quiet of late,' she added.

'I've been busy with work, and the African project. You know that.'

'So you've no girlfriend?'

'No.' It wasn't a lie and yet it felt like one. Rachel seemed to have taken up residence in his brain whether or not they were technically seeing each other. As if she belonged there. He shook his head.

'A mother knows, you know, and I

suspect there's someone in the wings. I see can it in your face, dear.'

Grant decided to change the subject and tell his mother how the project was going. 'You know I'll be in Africa soon? In seven weeks, actually.'

She nodded but continued with her knitting.

Of course she knew. It was completely the wrong time to be bringing a significant other into his life.

9

The taxi ended up in a small queue of ball-goers, all being dropped off at the main entrance of The Carlton, one of the smartest hotels in town. A doorman in livery indicated which direction to take but it was easy just to follow the trail of black-jacketed men and ladies in all kinds of finery.

Rachel had chosen a black and silver dress she'd had for a while and had worn to a medical school ball or two, but teamed it with a new necklace and new heels. It had been a rush, getting away from the hospital and back to her flat to change in time, but now she was here she started to relax.

There was nothing else to do this evening but sit back and enjoy herself. Even if she didn't know anyone but Kate at the table, The Carlton boasted a well-known chef so the food was bound to beat a night in with a ready meal.

She took a glass of champagne from an offered tray and then suddenly saw a familiar face. 'Tina! What are you doing here?'

Tina Holland turned around. 'Hi, Rachel. Actually my father is involved with the charity. I didn't realise you were coming, or of course I'd have invited you to join our table.' Tina looked a little abashed.

Rachel discovered why a moment later as Dr Stuart Thorpe, the other F2 who was currently doing his rotation in maternity, came over carrying two drinks. From the look that passed between him and Tina it was clear they had a relationship outside of work.

'Dr Booth, can I get you a drink?' he offered.

'No I'm fine for now.' She indicated her glass of champagne.

Stuart gave a small smile but seemed a little awkward. 'Is your father here yet, Tina?' he said.

It suddenly occurred to Rachel that Tina's father might be the eminent Professor Holland. He worked at one of the London teaching hospitals as far as Rachel could remember but had published many notable papers in Obstetrics. 'Is your father . . . I mean . . . ?'

'Yes, he's Professor Holland.' Tina took a sip of her drink. 'I didn't mention it before it in case it clouded anyone's judgement of me. I'll introduce you, though, if you'd like to meet him?'

'Of course,' Rachel said. 'I've read lots of his papers and there is one in particular I'd like to ask him about.'

'And obviously tell him how brilliantly I'm doing at City Hospital.'

'Naturally.' Rachel laughed and gave Stuart a conspiratorial wink.

* * *

Grant gave everyone he was introduced to at least three or four minutes of his undivided attention. You never knew who might be interested in donating and, after all, that was what this entire evening was all about.

After an hour he was starting to feel exhausted. Surely it couldn't be much longer until dinner was served? He excused himself from the small group he was with and walked over towards the bar, ignoring a waiter with a tray of champagne.

'Soda water, please,' he said to the barman.

He leaned on the chrome and copper bar and surveyed the scene. The room which had been empty when he'd arrived was now full and the conversation buzzing. Undoubtedly a good idea to serve champagne on arrival; although it meant they'd make a little less on the tickets, if it set a few people up in the right mood for the charity auction later, they might raise a significant sum of money.

And then he saw her. Wearing a silvery dress that skimmed her figure to her hips before falling to her ankles. Nothing immodest about it, and yet . . .

146

She had her hand on the arm of some man. It was that student doctor, Dr Thorpe. Grant felt himself frowning. What was Rachel doing here anyway? He'd not told her about the project.

The barman set down his soda water on a paper mat in front of him.

Rachel tossed her head back and laughed. She was standing in a little group with Dr Thorpe, the other F2, Dr Holland and an older man he didn't recognise. She'd removed her hand from Thorpe's arm but they still all looked very friendly together.

Grant picked up his glass and drained it. The cold ice hit his teeth and his hand tightened around the glass. It was something primitive, but he didn't like seeing her with another man. He set the glass down carefully and took a deep breath.

'Ladies and gentlemen, please take your seats for dinner.' The maître d' gestured and seemed to get the room's attention straight away.

'See you later,' Tina said and left with

Stuart and the Professor, leaving Rachel in the middle of a throng that was moving towards the second half of the room packed with round dinner tables. She hadn't checked the seating plan and so didn't even know if she was heading in the right direction. She looked around hoping to spot Kate.

A hand rested on her shoulder and Rachel jumped back.

'Only me.' Grant Mackenzie, looking implausibly handsome in his dinner suit, stood next to her.

'Is the whole hospital here tonight?' Rachel murmured. Despite her heart beating wildly in her chest and her stomach feeling like jelly, she wasn't even sure if she was happy to see him.

'I hope not.' Grant sounded very serious. 'Especially not Maria.'

Rachel couldn't help smiling. 'But she's so fond of you.'

'She's fond of everyone male.' He picked her hand up and lifted it to his lips. 'Enchanted to see you too, Dr Booth.'

Rachel snatched her hand away but it was too late to stop the tingle from his touch cascading up her arm and down her spine. How dare he try to provoke feelings in her he wasn't prepared to follow through! He was the one who'd cooled initially, but then there had been all those flowers and then nothing again. And now here he was, flirting with her again.

'Excuse me, I must find my table.'

'Which is?' His smile seemed to demand a response.

Rachel wanted to walk away but she couldn't. There was nothing to do but confess. 'Actually I don't know. I didn't look at the plan.'

Grant's smile widened. 'Let me help — '

'No, it's quite all right.' She swung away, desperate to put physical distance between them, but he was too close, too demanding.

'Rachel! Rachel, there you are.' Kate Prosser came towards her. 'Oh Grant! I didn't know you knew Rachel.'

'Very well, actually.' Grant had stopped smiling but his eyes still sparkled with a touch of mischief. 'We work together.'

Rachel stared at the floor, hoping it might swallow her up. No such luck.

'Of course, at the hospital,' Kate said. 'Well, what a surprise. Rachel's my neighbour and I invited her, so she's on our table.'

'Wonderful.' Grant sounded sincere. Which was worse. Sarcastic would have been better. Disinterested, better still. She could deal with those. 'Let's go and eat, then,' he added chirpily.

Rachel gripped her clutch bag tightly and followed them to a table in the middle of the room. She didn't recognise any of their fellow diners. Patrons of the charity, she supposed, and she understood now why Kate had been keen to invite her as there was only two other ladies on the table, both older.

'What a coincidence, us both working with Grant,' Kate said. 'Now would you like to sit here, Rachel?' She gestured to an empty seat.

'You work at City Hospital, too?' Rachel was puzzled. She was sure Kate had said she worked for the charity this ball was in aid of, but perhaps it was only part-time.

'Oh, no, not at the hospital — for the charity.' Kate gave a wide smile. 'Oh, did you not know that Grant . . . '

'Is that my name I hear?' Grant pulled out a chair for her and Rachel had no option but to sit down.

'I'll sit here, next to our honoured guest.' Grant sat down next to her.

Rachel reached for the menu and pretended to study it. Just the fact that he was sitting next to her made her feel enclosed and that she suddenly wanted to escape. This was supposed to be an evening off, not an ordeal. She took in a deep breath. She could normally handle anything, but Grant seemed to have this strangely disconcerting effect on her.

'Kate said you worked together?' she asked politely.

'Yes.' Grant offered her some mineral water.

'So you work for this charity as well as the hospital?' Rachel pressed.

'Well, not really, more just giving some directional advice.' He sounded dismissive or uninterested, Rachel couldn't tell which.

Luckily, Kate placed another doctor on her other side. James Nelson was in paediatrics at Granby General and they soon struck up a conversation. Rachel stole a glance to see if Grant had noticed, but he was talking with the woman on his right.

A waitress came round with their starters, dainty mozzarella and bacon salads drizzled with pesto.

'Looks good,' Grant remarked.

'Great, because I'm starving,' James Nelson added. 'Good turnout tonight, Mackenzie, you must be pleased.'

'Of course, but it's Kate and the team who have done all the hard work.' Grant smiled at Kate across the table and Rachel felt something shrivel in her chest. Not jealousy, surely? She wasn't jealous of Kate Prosser. Grant could smile at whoever he liked.

'Such a worthwhile project,' Dr Nelson mused. 'I've spoken to the team about possibly getting our whole department involved in some fund-raising.'

'Kate's your woman, then,' Grant said.

'Dr Nelson, that sounds fabulous,' Kate said from across the table. Grant smiled at her and she smiled back. Rachel wanted to be somewhere else far away. She should have known that Grant Mackenzie was bad news from the moment they first met. Grant and his 'complicated' life. Well, she saw it for what it was now. The complication was Kate Prosser.

Rachel took a sip of her wine and as she put the glass down again she realised that Grant was staring at her. A tingling feeling went down her spine. She tried to ignore it and picked up her knife and fork. She didn't care about him any more. And she'd tell herself that one thousand times over until she finally made herself believe it.

Somehow, and with the help of James Nelson and general conversation around the table, she got through dinner and then coffee while the auction was held. As the auctioneer announced the grand total raised for the charity, she breathed a sigh of relief. Soon the dancing would start and she would no longer be trapped sitting here within six inches of a man who unsettled her just by existing. If she'd known how this evening was going to turn out, she'd never have come.

'So when are you off to Africa?' James Nelson suddenly asked Grant.

'In about seven weeks.'

Rachel caught his eye and he appeared to look a little uncomfortable. What was it to her if he was off on holiday to Africa? She really must stop thinking about him in any way expect as a work colleague.

'And how long are you out there for?' Dr Nelson persisted.

Grant chewed his lip. 'At least six months.'

'Excuse me,' Rachel said and stood up, pushing her chair back a little too violently so that she had to turn around and catch hold of it.

She couldn't look at him. Six months! Thanks for nothing, Grant Mackenzie. Just as well their relationship had hardly got started. He was going away to Africa. No wonder he'd not wanted to get involved.

She couldn't look at anyone. She was surrounded by chatter, the noise of people enjoying themselves, yet the room seemed a blur and she kept on walking. She pushed open the door to the ladies' cloakroom.

'I am pathetic,' she muttered to herself as she hid in one of the posh cubicles. She perched on the closed toilet seat and leaned her head against the cool wall. It was like she had some kind of schoolgirl crush that had nothing to do with reality.

Grant must have known for a while

that he was off to Africa and it was one very good reason why he'd not want to get involved with anyone. *Pull yourself together*, Rachel instructed herself and reminded herself that she was a grown-up, a qualified professional and that all she had to do now was stay at a charity ball for another hour and look as if she was enjoying the evening before she could jump in a taxi home. Home to cry.

She ventured out and touched up her lipstick. She gave herself a long, hard look in the mirror and returned to the ballroom.

'Hi! Listen, Rachel . . . er . . . ' Grant was waiting for her — as if he would be loitering outside the cloakrooms for any other reason.

'Perhaps another time?' Rachel struggled to stay cool and collected.

'About Africa — '

'Yes, good film I seem to recall. Meryl Streep — '

'Listen for a moment.' Grant ran a hand through his hair. 'It's not what you think. Anyway, that was *Out of Africa*.'

'I'm pretty sure it is exactly as I think. But that's fine. Grant, I understand now why you were so keen to cool it.'

'All right then.' He stuffed his hands in his pockets. 'No, wait a moment, it's not all right. Look, when can I see you?'

'I'm standing right in front of you.'

'To talk about this properly. We need to talk. I need to explain.'

'Sorry, Grant, there's nothing to say.' Rachel stared at the plush carpet on the floor. 'You don't owe me any explanations. See you around.'

She started to move away from him as fast as she could without looking like a fool. She found herself heading for the bar, which seemed as good place as any.

Tina and Stuart were there. Any friendly face was perfect right now. Rachel's chest was heavy and she was breathing far too fast. She felt a little lightheaded and it was unpleasant.

'What will you have, boss?' Tina said.

'Vodka and tonic would be lovely, thanks.' Perhaps she shouldn't be drinking. 'On second thoughts, just a tomato juice with Worcester sauce.'

'Sure thing, Dr Booth.' Stuart turned to the barman and ordered.

'So how are things going?' Rachel asked Tina while Stuart was busy.

'Anything you want to raise with me off-duty?'

'You make it sound like it's my appraisal,' Tina replied. 'But thanks for asking. No, you're a great mentor and I'm sorry I won't be with you much longer — my rotation's up at the end of the month.'

'So what will you miss most?'

Tina grinned. 'Queuing up to get your coffee every morning.'

Rachel grinned too. 'I never asked you to fetch my coffee every morning.'

'Okay, yes, I made a rod for my own back, but you're always so grateful when you arrive in the office and it's there on your desk waiting.'

'Excuse me.' Grant was suddenly upon them. 'Rachel, I believe you promised me this dance.'

'Oh, Dr Thorpe's just got me a drink.' She picked her tomato juice up from the bar.

'What would you like?' Stuart pulled his wallet out again. 'You work at City Hospital, don't you?'

'Yes, yes, I do. Nothing for me, thank you.' Grant seemed to be speaking through his teeth and his eyes flashed. Surely he wasn't . . . ? He couldn't be . . . Jealous? Jealous of Stuart Thorpe? No, what a silly idea.

'If you'll excuse us, then.' Tina and Stuart sidled away.

'What did you do that for?' Rachel turned on Grant and tried to control her anger. She rarely got angry but her emotions were on a knife edge and everything Grant did or said seemed to make her feel worse.

'Do what?'

'You know exactly what I mean. You're standing there looking like thunder and now they've gone off, embarrassed probably.'

Grant pressed his lips together. 'Because you and I hadn't finished our earlier conversation.'

'We had. There's nothing more to say.'

'You'll listen to me.' Grant placed his hand on her arm. She shook it away. 'Okay, okay, let's dance, then,' he said. 'Then we'll talk.'

Rachel decided not to argue. Something told her that when Grant was in a mood to be persistent he wasn't going to leave her alone any time soon.

The band were playing popular hits from different decades but as they reached the dance floor they started a slow dance and only couples stayed on the dance floor.

'Come on.' Grant gathered her into his arms. He spoke so close to her ear that she could feel his breath warm on her cheek. A pleasant shiver ran down her spine.

Rachel bit her lip and draped her

arms across his broad shoulders.

They swayed in time to the music and she found herself losing her sense of time and place as she sank into his warmth. She might be anywhere in the world but it only mattered that she was with Grant.

Oh, how she wished he felt the same way about her; that he wasn't going away to Africa, that things had been different. Just the thought made her want to cry. She opened her eyes wide and looked about to prevent the tears from coming.

They were one of only half a dozen couples dancing. Not that they were actually a couple. Rachel was somewhat relieved when the slow dance ended and the band went back to playing something upbeat. Grant's physical proximity just made what might have been seem so much worse.

'Dance, or talk?' Grant continued to hold her hands and if she were being honest with herself, she didn't want him to let them go.

'Talk,' she whispered. She wasn't in the mood for disco dancing.

Grant ushered her to an empty table and they sat down. Rachel folded her hands in her lap and watched him while he picked up a stray teaspoon and began to turn it over between his fingers. Rachel wanted to reach out and place her hand on his, to touch him, to comfort him perhaps. But it didn't seem the right thing to do at this moment.

Grant was obviously tense and she hoped, but also feared, that she was about to find out why.

'Rachel, I don't know how to say this . . . ' he began, raking his hands through his hair. 'I never intended when we first started seeing each other that it would be like this.'

'What do you mean?' Rachel held her breath.

He looked her directly in the eye. 'That I would have feelings for you . . . such strong feelings . . . '

'Isn't that always the risk when you

162

start seeing someone?'

'It's never happened to me before. Perhaps at the time I thought it did, but not when I look back.' Grant spoke quietly. 'Not like this . . . '

Rachel listened to every one of her own breaths as the silence stretched before them. She could hardly believe what she was hearing and she couldn't think of anything to say.

Grant had feelings for her. He did care in his own way, whatever that meant. 'I have feelings for you too,' she eventually murmured, surprised even at her own words.

'You see.' Grant gave a rueful smile and shrugged. 'We're in a right mess, aren't we?'

'Because you're going to Africa?'

'Yes.' Grant stared at the floor.

'But that's weeks away, isn't it?' She didn't really want to think about it.

'Six weeks. I finish my contract at City Hospital in five. Not so long.'

'Well then, we should make the most of the time we do have left, shouldn't we?' Rachel said. Grant stared at her strangely and, emboldened the words tumbled from her in a rush. 'Come back to mine,' she said.

It was perhaps the boldest thing she had ever said in her life — and it hung between them like unclaimed washing on a line. Rachel looked into his eyes and defied him to say no. They both knew what was likely to happen if they went back to her flat and her whole body tingled just thinking about it. She knew she couldn't have him for the long term, or even the medium term, but she could have him now.

She tried not to think about how she was going to feel when he did go. For once in her life, she needed to just live for the moment.

'No.' Grant looked away and shook his head.

'Right . . . okay . . . well, erm . . . ' She should go. Now.

'See you on Monday?' he asked flatly.

'At work?' Her heart didn't know whether to leap or plummet.

'Perhaps we could grab a coffee, or a quick breakfast together?' He stared at his hands, flexing his fingers backwards and forwards. 'I'd like for us to still be friends . . . '

'I don't think so, Grant.' She really couldn't take this any longer, his blowing hot and cold on her. She just wanted to go home now. Alone.

While she was still able to keep herself together, she pushed her chair back and stood up. ''Bye, then.'

* * *

Grant watched her go with a mixture of relief and frustration. Relief that at least now she knew why he'd acted as he had. But at the same time it didn't feel good. No, it didn't feel good at all. Perhaps his mother was right and he'd never be any good at relationships until he was happy with the rest of his life. And yet, he was happy — or rather, he should be happy. He was getting everything he wanted. Every day the hospital in Tanzania was coming closer to reality. The Andrew Mackenzie Hospital — he could see the signage in his mind's eye.

He pulled at his collar and fiddled with one of his cufflinks. He had wanted to chase after her, but he didn't have that luxury. He had a duty here, this evening, a duty that the lives of ordinary people in Africa might rest upon. He had better get back to his guests; dinner would be finishing soon and then he was due to make his appeal speech.

Later, back at the executive apartment he'd rented on a short lease, he made straight for the large silver-framed photograph that stood on the hall table — the first thing visitors noticed on entering the flat.

It was a picture of two brothers together; him and Andrew. He must have been about eighteen when it was taken, and he was relaxed and carefree. Even Andrew looked relaxed — it was perhaps the only photo of Andrew where he didn't look focussed and serious.

Suddenly Grant realised that he had placed Andrew there to keep an eye on him; a constant reminder of what had been lost and what he was working towards. Well, no longer, he told himself.

When he wondered what Andrew would have made of it all, when he really thought about it, he didn't like the answer. No doubt Andrew the doctor would have supported the idea as much as anyone with an ounce of humanity would have — but Andrew the man? What if their roles had been reversed? Would Andrew have gone out to Africa himself to supervise the build, to work there in person?

No, Andrew had wanted a glittering career as a surgeon and he wouldn't have taken much time, if any, from the path towards that. He'd have put up his money, certainly, but he'd have delegated the job to someone else.

They might have been brothers but

Grant had to accept that Andrew was a different personality, more driven, more ruthless, in some ways less empathetic. For the first time Grant found himself speculating as to Andrew's motivations for becoming a doctor in the first place.

No, Andrew wasn't perfect but still, he hadn't deserved to die. Grant placed the photograph face down on the table. He needed to find a less obtrusive home for it, but that would do for now.

Grant brooded all weekend. From whichever angle he thought about things he kept coming back to the same conclusion — he'd give up Africa for Rachel. His mother was right, after all. He had it bad and he'd never felt like this before.

By Monday morning he was determined to talk to Rachel — if she'd let him. Well, she jolly well would let him, he decided, even if he had to lock her in the ward pantry to make her listen.

10

Rachel breezed into her office and was surprised to see her usual coffee wasn't waiting for her on her desk. Oh dear, she really had been taking Tina's good nature for granted. Granted . . . Grant . . .

She threw her handbag down next to her chair. She'd have to see him today, no doubt they'd bump into each other at some point. She could deal with it. She was professional.

She sat down and turned her computer on. She'd just check her emails and then grab a coffee before the morning clinic.

The door opened and she looked up to see it was Tina. Why did she keep expecting Grant to appear at every moment?

'Hi, sorry I'm late,' Tina said. She was carrying two coffees and put one down in front of Rachel.

'Thanks — but late? The clinic's not until half nine.'

'Late for me, then. You know me, keen and all that.' She smiled.

'It was nice to meet your dad.' Rachel opened the lid of the plastic coffee cup to let it cool a little. 'Did you enjoy the rest of the night?'

'A few of us went on from the ball on Friday to a club,' Tina said. 'And we met up by chance with some folks from here. So, yeah, it was a good night. Did you go home quite early from the ball?' Tina frowned. 'I don't remember seeing you later.'

'I'd had a long week. I was tired.'

'You know I was really surprised to see Grant Mackenzie at the ball.' Tina sat down at the F2's desk. 'But then I remembered he's not exactly an ordinary midwife after it all came out in the papers when he delivered that woman in the lift.'

'No.' Rachel stared at her emails. She didn't want to talk about Grant.

'But I was amazed when I found out

all about how the whole charity was his idea. It's going to be called after his brother, the one who died tragically.'

'Really?' Rachel remarked. It was all starting to make sense now. Grant had trained to be a midwife in order to have useful skills to take to Africa, and he needed to qualify in time. It was not madness, it was part of a big, well thought out game plan.

Grant was a hotbed of secrets, but none of them made her like him any less. If anything . . . no, she didn't want to think like that now. It was too late.

'People are just full of surprises,' Tina said. 'Like when Stu — Dr Thorpe — suddenly asked me out one day while we were reviewing an ultrasound!'

'You certainly kept that one quiet.' Rachel smiled.

'Well . . . ' Tina took a swig of her coffee. 'Let's say Dr Thorpe and I are definitely an item.'

'Well, congratulations!' Rachel heard the beep of her phone battery dying and fished in her bag for it. 'You don't happen to have a charger lying about, do you? I forgot to charge my phone up.'

Tina rifled through her handbag. 'Might have, though I dunno if it will fit.'

Rachel noticed a new text message had come through, *Still on for lunch 2day? Becks xxx*

Oh no, she'd arranged to meet Becky before she'd swapped some shifts around. Becky had started her maternity leave last week was probably expecting a girls' lunch in the city centre followed by a bit of shopping.

She typed quickly before the battery died. *Working today but could grab quick bite. Can u come to City Hosp for 1pm? R xxx*

A moment later the reply appeared. *Sure. C u then. B xxx*

'Sorry, no charger.' Tina shook her head. 'But I'll ask around for you.'

'Great, you're a star.'

★ ★ ★

Rachel leaned over the midwives' station to deposit some notes. She'd had to leave Tina covering for her last half hour of the clinic because the labour ward was overflowing. She'd just checked on two mothers in second stage and one was almost certainly going to need an assisted delivery. Maria, the Spanish midwife, was getting the team together right now.

'Dr Booth!' An Irish midwife whose name Rachel had forgotten came running down the corridor from Antenatal. 'Have you got a moment to have a look at a trace?'

'Yes, okay, but can you bring it to me? I'm going to Labour Room Eight for an assisted delivery.'

'Right you are.' The midwife scurried off again.

What a morning! Rachel took a mint from the packet in her pocket and turned on her heels towards the labour rooms. She could do with a biscuit really, but there was no time.

The double doors burst open and a

trolley rattled through guided by two porters — and Grant! Rachel looked away and started to head off.

'Dr Booth!' Grant's voice. 'We have an emergency.'

'Page the on-call consultant,' Rachel called to the student midwife who was lurking behind the midwives' station. She couldn't be in two places at once. She glanced up at the board. 'Labour Ward's completely full. Let's take her into Antenatal.'

She quickly glanced at the mother on the trolley. It was Becky! 'Becky? Becks, what happened?'

'I tried calling you . . . ' Becky's voice sounded weak.

'She's lost a lot of blood,' Grant said.

'What are you? Thirty-one weeks?' Don't say her sister was in labour at thirty-one weeks! Please, no!

Becky nodded. 'I've had pains in my lower back but I just thought it was backache, you know. But then this morning the bleeding started.'

They went into the first free Antenatal side room. 'Let's get a trace,' Rachel instructed. Grant wheeled the machine over and got it set up while Rachel listened to the baby using the handheld monitor. The heartbeat was initially strong, but then it began to slow down. Rachel felt her throat constrict. She knew it was foetal distress.

'Oh no, oh no . . . ' Becky shook her head from side to side.

'Listen, Becks, we've got a consultant coming as I shouldn't really be treating you, as you're my sister, but we have to deliver the baby now.'

Grant rushed out of the room without even being asked. Whatever else he was, he was a first class midwife. She hadn't even needed to utter the words 'emergency C-section' and he knew what to do.

Tears started to roil down Becky's cheeks. 'Oh no, no . . . '

Rachel took her hand. 'Is Jamie on his way? Do you want me to call?'

'I already called him, but he's going

to miss it, isn't he?'

'I'm afraid so.'

'Oh, Rach, I can't believe this is happening. The baby is going to be all right, isn't it?'

'The odds at thirty-one weeks are excellent. It's going to be fine.' Rachel bit her lip. Now wasn't the time to go into the myriad of possible complications there might be.

A trolley rattled noisily into the room, pushed by Grant.

'Can't you come with me?' Becky gripped Rachel's hand as if her life depended on it.

'I can't, but I'll be right here, waiting for you.'

'I'll come with you into theatre,' Grant reassured her. 'I'll be there every step of the way. Now, let's get you onto this beauty of a trolley.'

'You're in good hands,' Rachel said — and she meant it. She'd seen Grant at work so many times now and even when the pressure was on, he was an excellent midwife. She flashed Grant a grateful smile but he appeared not to notice.

She was glad. He was concentrating on doing his job.

* ★ ★

Jamie arrived five minutes later looking as if he'd run the whole way across town in his office suit, with his shirt untucked and tie askew.

'She's in theatre. The baby is being delivered now.'

'Oh, right.' Jamie looked confused and Rachel didn't blame him. It wasn't just a shock to the mother to have your baby arrive so early.

Right on cue they heard the unmistakable cry of a newborn.

'Is that . . . ?' Jamie dragged his hand across his brow.

'Yes.' Rachel couldn't help smiling. 'Look, shall we get a coffee? I might wear this corridor out otherwise. Becks needs to wake up from the general anaesthetic and the baby will be taken to the neonatal intensive care unit. Let's give everyone ten minutes and then we'll head to NICU.'

Rachel didn't mention that the little one was likely to need oxygen and could well be quite poorly.

'Okay. Gosh, I think this is all still just starting to sink in.'

'Are you expecting a boy or a girl?'

'We don't know. Becks wanted it to be a surprise.'

Dr Larsson came out of the theatre. 'Is this the father?' Rachel nodded. 'Congratulations, sir, you're the father of a baby girl. Now, because she's premature she'll be in the care of the neonatal team who are checking her over. She came out breathing on her own, however, which is an excellent sign. You should be able to see her shortly.'

'Thank you,' Jamie muttered. He had broken out in a cold sweat but now he looked as if he might even smile.

Rachel touched his arm. 'Come on, we need that celebratory coffee.'

She was used to holding it together, staying calm when the pressure was on. It was always afterwards, when she stopped being Dr Booth and was just Rachel again, that things hit her.

She stared at the tiny baby in NICU. Her own sister's child; she was now an auntie. She expected feelings as to what might have been had Russell not left her to come flooding in but, strangely, they didn't. Or at least, not yet. She was simply filled with awe at this tiny being, and lots of love.

Jamie stared at his baby. Rachel couldn't begin to imagine what he was thinking. After some time had passed in silence, she suggested he take a photo with his phone to show Becky. And all of a sudden, she was a medical professional again, dishing out advice she'd never had to take herself.

She guided Jamie to the postnatal high dependency unit to see Becky and after a brief greeting to her sister, slunk away to leave them together.

She hoped her office was empty. It was and she sank unto her chair. She was crying when she heard a knock on the door. Pulling a tissue quickly from her handbag, she wiped her eyes and called out, 'Come in.'

'I thought I'd find you here,' Grant said. He closed the door behind him.

'Sorry.' Rachel got up and dropped the tissue in the bin.

'You wouldn't be human if you felt any differently.' Grant's voice was soft and soothing and suddenly his arms were around her and then there was nothing she could do except sob into his shoulder.

'Little baby Becky is breathing on her own,' he said encouragingly.

'Really?' That was good news. 'Gosh, I'm sorry.' Rachel pulled herself away and tried to ignore the feeling that leaning on his warm, solid shoulder was the only place she wanted to be in the world. 'I should be more professional . . . I mean . . . '

'Rachel, she's your sister.'

'I know that, but . . . '

'Just forget for the moment that you're a doctor.'

Rachel didn't reply — not that there was anything smart or useful she had ready to say anyway.

Grant's hand brushed her cheek and she looked up into eyes that were watching her intently. 'You are exactly the sort of person to be the mother of my children,' he said with a wry smile.

Rachel felt her heart start to beat wildly.

He lowered his head and his lips met hers and she was in another place, where all that mattered was the touch of his lips and the feel of his hand on her cheek. Far, far away from this hospital and this city, under the blazing skies of Africa.

She had no idea how long their kiss lasted, only that when it ended, she never wanted to be apart from him again. He held her hands in his own and, if anything, he seemed a little nervous.

'Will you come with me to Africa?' he said. 'I'm building a hospital there in memory of my brother. I thought it might be the best thing I might do with my life but now I know I'm wrong. You're the best thing in my life and I never want to let you go.'

'Yes, I'd go anywhere with you,' Rachel sighed and kissed him again.

THE END

We do hope that you have enjoyed reading this large print book.

Did you know that all of our titles are available for purchase?

We publish a wide range of high quality large print books including:
Romances, Mysteries, Classics
General Fiction
Non Fiction and Westerns

Special interest titles available in large print are:
The Little Oxford Dictionary
Music Book, Song Book
Hymn Book, Service Book

Also available from us courtesy of Oxford University Press:
Young Readers' Dictionary
(large print edition)
Young Readers' Thesaurus
(large print edition)

For further information or a free brochure, please contact us at:
Ulverscroft Large Print Books Ltd.,
The Green, Bradgate Road, Anstey,
Leicester, LE7 7FU, England.
Tel: (00 44) **0116 236 4325**
Fax: (00 44) **0116 234 0205**

TAKE A CHANCE ON ME

Teresa Ashby

A marathon brings doctors Anna Curtis and Riordan 'Mac' McKenna together. Anna has moved into the area with her late sister's little boy, Cameron, and Mac offers her a job at his surgery. They become close and Anna falls pregnant. However, when Mac's ex-wife informs her that he doesn't want children, she decides she must move away. Can Mac finally convince her that he loves her, Cameron and the baby?

LOVE IS ALL AROUND

Beth James

When Holly and Granny Jean embark on a round-Britain cruise, Holly little expects to meet up with Ben. Accompanying his grandad, he's wildly attractive, but annoyingly confident. However, after a bad start, Holly is drawn, irresistibly, to a more likeable side to Ben. But Grandad is grumpy, whilst Granny Jean is determinedly cheerful — and the entertainment hostess is more than a little interested in Ben. Holly is left wondering if this is good or bad!

JOURNEY TO PARADISE

Dawn Bridge

Lauren is on holiday in the Bahamas when a tropical storm breaks out. She is left in the care of Glenn, a very attractive American who takes shelter with her. They fall in love — but the problem is, he is the boyfriend of her best friend Anna. Lauren returns home racked with guilt, vowing to forget Glenn, but he has other ideas. Can they find a way of being together without hurting Anna?